To my … py Kid.

Xm …

Love Dad.

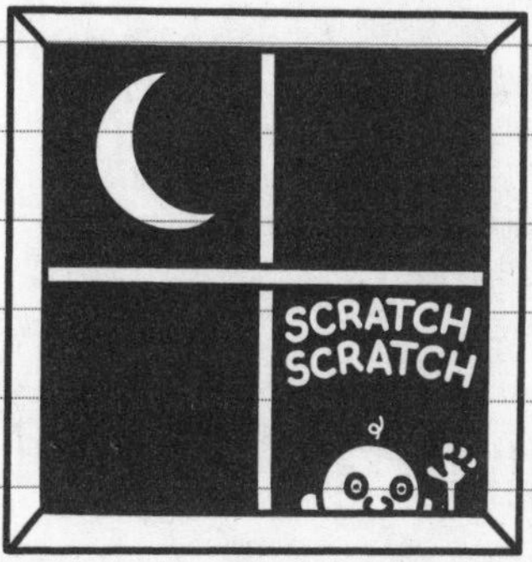

OTHER BOOKS BY JEFF KINNEY

Diary of a Wimpy Kid

Diary of a Wimpy Kid: Rodrick Rules

Diary of a Wimpy Kid: The Last Straw

Diary of a Wimpy Kid: Dog Days

Diary of a Wimpy Kid: The Ugly Truth

The Wimpy Kid Do-It-Yourself Book

The Wimpy Kid Movie Diary

COMING SOON

More *Diary of a Wimpy Kid*

DIARY of a Wimpy Kid

CABIN FEVER

by Jeff Kinney

PUFFIN BOOKS

PUFFIN BOOKS

Published by the Penguin Group
Penguin Group (Australia)
250 Camberwell Road, Camberwell, Victoria 3124, Australia
(a division of Pearson Australia Group Pty Ltd)
Penguin Group (USA) Inc.
375 Hudson Street, New York, New York 10014, USA
Penguin Group (Canada)
90 Eglinton Avenue East, Suite 700, Toronto, Canada ON M4P 2Y3
(a division of Pearson Penguin Canada Inc.)
Penguin Books Ltd
80 Strand, London WC2R 0RL England
Penguin Ireland
25 St Stephen's Green, Dublin 2, Ireland
(a division of Penguin Books Ltd)
Penguin Books India Pvt Ltd
11 Community Centre, Panchsheel Park, New Delhi – 110 017, India
Penguin Group (NZ)
67 Apollo Drive, Rosedale, Auckland 0632, New Zealand
(a division of Pearson New Zealand Ltd)
Penguin Books (South Africa) (Pty) Ltd
24 Sturdee Avenue, Rosebank, Johannesburg 2196, South Africa

Penguin Books Ltd, Registered Offices: 80 Strand, London, WC2R 0RL, England

First published in 2011 by Amulet Books, an imprint of Abrams
First published by Penguin Group (Australia), 2011

3 5 7 9 10 8 6 4

Cover design by Chad W. Beckerman and Jeff Kinney
Book design by Jeff Kinney
Colour separation by Splitting Image Colour Studio, Clayton, Victoria
Printed and bound in Australia by McPherson's Printing Group, Maryborough, Victoria

Cataloguing-in-Publication data has been applied for and may
be obtained from the National Library of Australia

ISBN: 978 0 14 330664 1

puffin.com.au

TO TICHINO

Saturday

Most people look forward to the holidays, but the stretch between Thanksgiving and Christmas just makes me a nervous wreck. If you make a mistake in the first eleven months of the year, it's no big deal. But if you do something wrong during the holiday season, you're gonna pay for it.

It's too much pressure to be on your best behavior for a whole month. The most I can really handle is six or seven days in a row. So if they moved Thanksgiving to the week before Christmas, it would be fine by me.

Kids whose families don't celebrate Christmas are lucky because they don't have to stress out whenever they do something wrong at this time of year. In fact, I have a few friends in that category who I think act a little extra jerky around now just because they can.

The thing that REALLY makes me nervous is this whole Santa issue. The fact that he can see you when you're sleeping and knows when you're awake really creeps me out. So I've started wearing sweatpants to bed because I really don't need Santa seeing me in my underwear.

I'm not really convinced that Santa has the time to keep an eye on you twenty-four hours a day anyway. I figure he can only check in on each kid once or twice a year for a few seconds—and with my luck, that happens at the most embarrassing moments.

If Santa really DOES see everything you do, then I could be in trouble. So when I write him, I don't say what I want for Christmas and all that. I use my letters to paint myself in the best possible light.

Dear Santa,
I did not throw a crab apple at Mrs. Taylor's cat, even though it might've looked that way from a distance.
Sincerely,
Greg Heffley

Then there's this "Naughty or Nice" list they're always talking about. You hear about it, but you never actually get to SEE it, so it's up to grown-ups to tell you where you stand at any given moment. And something about that just doesn't seem right.

IF YOU HELP ME WITH THESE GROCERIES, I'LL BET IT WILL BE JUST ENOUGH TO MAKE SANTA'S "NICE" LIST!

I kind of wonder how accurate the list really is anyway. There's a kid named Jared Pyle who lives up the street from me, and if there's ANYONE who deserves to be on the "Naughty" list, it's him. But last year he got a dirt bike for Christmas, so don't even ask me WHAT Santa was thinking on THAT one.

It's not just Santa I've got to worry about, either. Last year when Mom was going through some old boxes, she found a homemade doll from her childhood.

Mom said the doll is called "Santa's Scout" and that his job is to watch how kids behave and then report back to Santa at the North Pole.

Well, I'm not a fan of that idea. First of all, I think you have a right to privacy in your own home. And second, Santa's Scout gives me the willies.

I don't really buy the idea that this doll is feeding Santa information, but just in case, I try to be extra good whenever I'm in the same room as Santa's Scout.

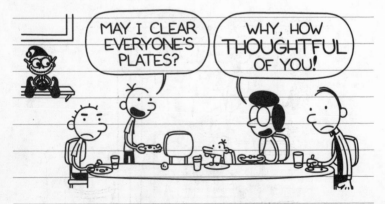

But it probably doesn't matter anyway, because my older brother, Rodrick, is constantly feeding Santa's Scout bad information about me.

I, GREG HEFFLEY, TOOK A TWENTY-DOLLAR BILL OUT OF MY MOTHER'S PURSE.

Every morning when I wake up, Santa's Scout is in a new place, which I guess is supposed to prove that he traveled to the North Pole overnight. But I'm starting to wonder if it's really Rodrick who moves him.

<u>Sunday</u>
Today we took all our Christmas decorations out
of the storage room in the basement. We have
boxes full of ornaments, and some of them are
pretty old. There's one with a picture of me and
Rodrick taking a bath in the sink that's really
embarrassing, but Mom won't let me throw it out.

We put up the tree in the living room and started
hanging ornaments on it. My little brother,
Manny, was taking a nap upstairs, and when he
woke up and found out we were decorating the
tree without him, he had a total meltdown.

The reason Manny was so upset was because someone hung his favorite ornament, this candy cane he really likes. So Mom took it off the tree and handed it to Manny to hang up himself.

But Manny wanted his ornament to be the FIRST one on the tree, so that meant we had to take all the decorations down, just so he could get his way.

And that's just the kind of thing that happens in my house every single day.

Mom hasn't started to use the threat of Santa as a way of getting Manny to behave, but I'm sure she will soon. I don't think it's such a good strategy for keeping us in line, though. Because the second Christmas is over, Mom doesn't have any real leverage.

WELL! THE EASTER BUNNY IS GOING TO BE **VERY** DISAPPOINTED IN YOU BOYS!

<u>Monday</u>

Right before Thanksgiving break, there was a contest at school to see who could come up with the best anti-bullying slogan, and the grand prize was a pizza party for the winning team.

Only YOU can STOP BULLYING!

Form a team of up to five people and come up with the best anti-bullying slogan. The winning team will get a PIZZA PARTY in the cafeteria! Let's make bullying extinct!

Everyone wanted that pizza party, and people didn't care WHAT they had to do to win it. Two groups of girls in my grade came up with slogans that were really similar, and each group accused the other one of stealing their idea.

The whole situation spun out of control, and eventually the vice principal had to step in to stop it from turning into a full-scale riot.

Our school only has one legitimate bully this year anyway, and his name is Dennis Root. And with all the signs and posters everywhere, I'm pretty sure the message is getting through to him.

The day before Thanksgiving there was a big anti-bullying assembly, and everyone in the auditorium was looking at Dennis the whole time. I kind of felt sorry for him, so I tried to make him feel better.

Even though Dennis is the only real bully in our school this year, we had a BUNCH of them LAST year. People were constantly getting picked on at recess, so the teachers set up a station on the playground where kids could press a button if they needed to get a grown-up's attention.

TELL-A-TEACHER
STATION

PRESS BUTTON
FOR HELP

Well, the Tell-a-Teacher station just ended up being a convenient place for the bullies to hang out and find their next victims.

The teachers say TEASING counts as bullying, too, but I don't think there's any way they're gonna put a stop to THAT. Kids are always calling each other names and that kind of thing at my school. In fact, one of the reasons I try to stay under the radar is because I don't want to end up getting stuck with a nickname like Cody Johnson did.

In kindergarten Cody stepped in some dog poop at recess, and ever since then people have called him "Dookie."

And I'm not just talking about the kids, either.
I'm talking about the teachers and even the
PRINCIPAL.

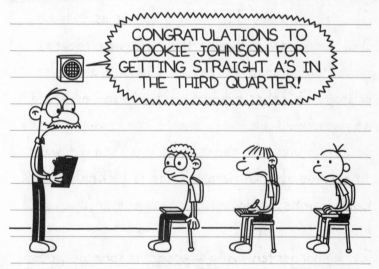

I'll tell you this: If I ever get a nickname like
Dookie, I'll move to a different town.

But what would probably happen is that someone from my OLD school would move to my new town and the whole thing would just start back up again.

The teachers always say that when you're getting picked on, you should tell an adult. I think that's a good idea, but it didn't work out so well when I was getting bullied.

There was this kid who lived in the neighborhood next to mine, and for some reason everyone called him "Nasty Pants."

Every time me and my friend Rowley went through Nasty Pants's neighborhood, he chased us with a stick.

The thing that really stunk was that me and Rowley used the woods in that neighborhood as a shortcut to get to school. So we started having to go out of our way to avoid getting harassed by Nasty Pants.

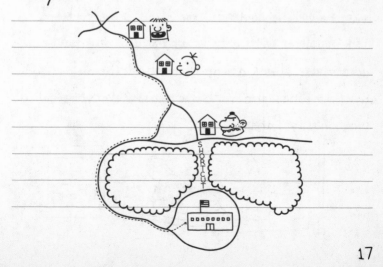

We did EXACTLY what the teachers are always telling us to do, and complained to the vice principal. But Vice Principal Roy said that since Nasty Pants didn't go to our school, there was nothing he could really do about it.

After getting chased a few more times, I decided I'd had enough, so I told Dad about the situation. I was afraid Dad was gonna say I needed to toughen up and deal with the problem myself, but he surprised me. Dad said that HE had problems with a bully at my age and he knew just what I was going through.

Dad's bully was named Billy Staples, and Billy's favorite thing to do was pin a kid's arm behind his back and hold it there until he cried.

Dad said that the kids in the neighborhood told their parents about Billy and they all went to Billy's house to confront his mom and dad. Mr. Staples made Billy promise to never pick on anyone ever again, and Dad said Billy burst into tears and might have even wet his pants.

Well, after hearing that story, I don't think Billy Staples would've been any match for Nasty Pants. But I told Dad I liked the idea of complaining to the bully's parents. I called up Rowley and told him to come over and to bring his dad, because we needed as much backup as we could get.

Dad knocked on Nasty Pants's door, and we waited for one of his parents to open it.

But Nasty Pants HIMSELF came to the door, and me and Rowley took off.

RAAAAH!

I guess I should've described Nasty Pants to Dad, because it took him a while to understand that the kid who came to the door was the one who was causing us all that trouble.

Dad talked to Mrs. Pants, and she told Dad her son was only five and that he just gets a little wound up sometimes.

YOU SMELL LIKE A DIRTY DIAPER. P.U.!

On the way home, Dad was pretty mad at me for letting myself get bullied by a kid who was still in kindergarten. But let me just say in my defense that when some kid is chasing you with a stick, you don't stop to ask him how old he is.

Tuesday

They took the last piece of playground equipment away at school today. We started off the year with all sorts of things, like monkey bars and swings and stuff, but now the playground is an empty sawdust pit.

So recess is basically like a prison yard.

I heard the school was having trouble paying the insurance for the playground, so every time there was some kind of accident or injury on a piece of equipment, the easiest thing to do was just remove it.

In October, Francis Knott went flying off the swing set and landed on the seesaw, so that took out two big items right there.

WAAUGH!

We lost the monkey bars when a girl named Christine Higgins climbed to the top and then got too scared to come down.

The teachers aren't allowed to touch kids, so they had to call Christine's parents to come and get her.

Eventually the only piece of equipment left was the balance beam, and I figured nobody could get hurt on THAT thing. But believe it or not, some idiot wasn't looking where he was going the other day, so now that's gone, too.

Without any playground equipment, there's really nothing for us to do. But the teachers won't even let us sit down, because they say we have to stay "active."

And it's not like you're allowed to bring in toys or video games to keep yourself occupied, either. In fact, if you get caught with a toy on the playground, it'll get confiscated. Last week somebody found a miniature car buried in the sawdust that looked like it had been there for years.

The car had three missing wheels, but people were so desperate for entertainment that they lined up to play with it while others kept lookout.

Now there's a black market for toys at our school. Christopher Stangel brought in a bunch of Legos from home yesterday, and I hear a single brick will set you back fifty cents.

The teachers have banned a bunch of games we used to play, too. Last week a group of boys were playing Freeze Tag, but one of them got hurt when someone shoved him from behind.

So now we're not allowed to touch each other or even RUN. Today people were playing "Air Tag" and getting around by speed-walking, but it wasn't really the same.

If you ask me, I think people are getting too carried away with all this safety stuff. I went to Manny's peewee soccer game, and all the kids had to wear bicycle helmets.

The only good thing about the playground equipment being gone is that now I actually have a chance to start doing well in school.

I'm one of those people who has a hard time focusing when the teacher is talking, and when another class is having recess right outside the window, it's practically impossible to pay attention.

Wednesday

OK, I take back what I said about being glad the playground equipment is gone. Now the kids at recess don't have anything to do, so they just stare in through the windows. And that's seriously distracting when you're trying to take a test.

It doesn't help that I'm not exactly the fastest test-taker. In third grade I had a teacher named Mrs. Sinclair who taught us all these great tricks for remembering multiplication facts. But they seriously slow me down.

♫ EIGHT TIMES FOUR IS THIRTY-TWO, ♫ THIRTY-TWO, THIRTY-TWO! ♩ EIGHT TIMES FOUR IS THIRTY-TWO, ♩ AND NOW YOU KNOW IT'S TRUE!

(TO THE TUNE OF "MARY HAD A LITTLE LAMB")

Earlier this year we had a math teacher named Mr. Sparks who used to stand on his chair every time he wanted us to remember something important.

But once when Mr. Sparks was trying to get us to remember a math concept, one of the legs on his chair broke and he fell.

Mr. Sparks broke his collarbone, and I heard he's suing the school over it. I don't remember the concept he was trying to teach us that day, but I do always remember never to stand on the furniture.

During recess today everyone was just waiting to go back inside, but then Rowley got up and started skipping around the playground.

A few people started cheering and clapping.
They must've thought Rowley was protesting all
the new rules by skipping instead of running, but
the truth is, skipping is just something Rowley
likes to do.

For some reason it really gets on my nerves when
Rowley skips, so it bugged me to see him prancing
around the playground like that. Skipping is
actually a real sore subject between the two of us.
Rowley says I'm jealous of him because I don't
know how to skip, but I think it just looks stupid.

I will admit that I never exactly got the hang of skipping. In fact, I was the only kid in first grade who couldn't do it.

I was afraid I'd be held back until I learned how to skip, but luckily they let me move on to second grade. Still, I'm worried it's gonna come back to haunt me later on.

Sometimes I wonder how me and Rowley ended up being friends in the first place, since we're so different. But at this point I figure we're stuck with each other, so I just try to overlook the things he does that annoy me.

Thursday

The thing that stinks about having Santa's Scout watching my every move at home is that I can't get away with the things I used to do during the holidays.

A few years ago Mom and Dad put some gifts under the tree a week before Christmas, and it was driving me crazy not knowing what they were.

SHAKE
SHAKE

One of the gifts had my name on it, and I was pretty sure it was a video game. I made a tiny little tear in the wrapping paper to see, and sure enough, it was a game I'd asked for.

But then it was bugging me that a game I wanted was sitting right there under the tree and I couldn't play it. So I went one step further and made a slit along the top of the packaging and slid the disc out.

I opened the plastic case and removed the game, then put the box back in the wrapping paper and taped it closed.

But I started to get paranoid that Mom was gonna pick up the present and notice it felt lighter, so I opened it back up and put one of Rodrick's heavy metal CDs inside the box to make it the same weight it was before.

I played the video game every night after Mom and Dad went to bed, and I actually beat it. But I forgot to put it back in the box, and on Christmas, when I opened my present in front of Mom and Dad, Rodrick's CD slipped out and rolled onto the floor.

The day after Christmas, Mom took the CD to the Game Hut and chewed the clerk out for selling her material that was "inappropriate" for kids.

I just don't like not knowing what I'm getting for Christmas, and sometimes I can't help myself. Last year I went on Mom's e-mail account and wrote to all our relatives to see if I could find out what they were getting me.

TO: Gammie, Uncle Joe, Uncle Charlie, Gramma, Grandpa, Uncle Gary, Joanne, Leslie, Byron, <u>23 more</u>

SUBJECT: Gifts

Hey, everyone—

Let me know what you're buying for Greg this year, so we can coordinate.

Thanks, Susan

But Mom keeps her e-mail on the computer in the kitchen, and it's hard to get onto her account when Santa's Scout is watching me like a hawk.

Tonight I spent some time trying to decide what to put on my Christmas wish list this year. I try to be as specific as possible when I make my list, because whenever I leave my gifts up to Mom and Dad, I get some crazy stuff.

A few years ago I forgot to write out a wish list, and I paid the price for it. Mom was pregnant with Manny, and she wanted me to get ready for having a baby brother.

So for Christmas, Mom got me a DOLL.

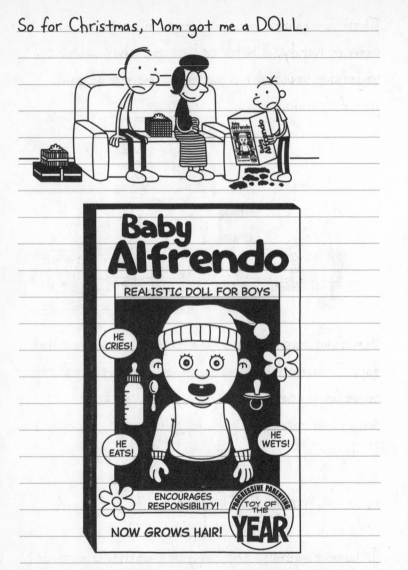

At first I didn't want anything to do with it.

Then I realized having a doll you could FEED came in handy. In fact, I don't think a vegetable touched my lips for a month after I got Alfrendo.

HERE COMES THE AIRPLANE, ALFRENDO! OPEN WIDE!

But that wasn't the only thing I used that doll for. I found out that he made a really excellent comic book stand, too.

I have to admit, after a few months I got really attached to that doll.

Since I didn't have a pet, it was kind of nice to have something to take care of for once.

But one day I came home from school and I couldn't find Alfrendo ANYWHERE. I searched the house from top to bottom, but there was no trace of him.

The only thing I could think of was that I dropped Alfrendo at some point and somehow didn't notice.

I was pretty torn up about losing my doll, but what I was REALLY worried about was Mom thinking I couldn't be trusted around my new baby brother. So I got a grapefruit out of the fridge and drew a face on it with a marker.

Then I wrapped the grapefruit in a dish towel, and for the next three months I pretended it was my doll.

ROCKABYE BABY ON THE TREETOP...

Mom and Dad didn't seem to notice. But I was terrified by the idea that the REAL Alfrendo was gonna find his way back home and get his revenge on me for abandoning him and replacing him with a fruit.

In fact, I still worry about that to this day. It's the reason I always check to make sure my window is locked before I go to bed at night.

I'm a little embarrassed to say this, but I actually got attached to that GRAPEFRUIT, too. But after a while it started to rot, and Dad traced the weird smell back to my Alfrendo decoy.

Mom didn't seem too upset that I'd lost my doll, but I will say she's never left me alone in the house with Manny for more than fifteen minutes.

Like I said, though, it was nice to have something to take care of, and I missed that feeling. So these days I've been spending a lot of time playing this game called Net Kritterz.

In fact, I've been playing Net Kritterz every free second I get. The basic idea is that you have to feed your pet and keep it happy. And if your pet is happy, you get tokens so you can buy it clothes and furniture and stuff like that.

I've played so much that my pet Chihuahua has a mansion with an indoor swimming pool, a bowling alley, and about 150 different outfits.

The only thing I'm not happy about is his NAME. Mom's the one who set up my account, and I can't figure out how to change the name she registered with.

GREGORY'S LITTLE FRIEND

Mom says I take better care of my virtual pet than I do MYSELF, and I guess I can't argue with her there. Over the weekend I played for sixteen hours without even taking a break to go to the bathroom.

But if you don't keep getting your pet new stuff, it starts to look unhappy, and that really stresses me out.

MOOD METER

GREGORY'S LITTLE FRIEND IS FEELING:

QUEASY

The problem is you can only earn a certain number of tokens, and after that you have to buy them with real money. Unfortunately, I don't have my own credit card, so that means I have to beg Mom and Dad to use THEIRS.

And it's not real easy to convince Dad to break open his wallet so you can buy a fancy outfit for your virtual pet.

MOOD METER

GREGORY'S LITTLE FRIEND IS FEELING:

SNAZZY

This year I'm gonna ask for a bunch of Kritterz Kash for Christmas. But I'm still trying to figure out what to put on the REST of my wish list. I could actually use a LOT of different things, because a couple weeks ago when I spent the night at the hospital getting my tonsils out, Manny sold half of everything I owned.

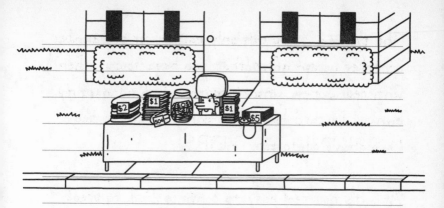

But I'm not so sure I should ask for a normal gift like a video game or a toy this year. What I've realized is that every time you get something cool for your birthday or for Christmas, within a week it's being used against you.

WE'LL BE TAKING THIS AWAY UNTIL YOUR ENGLISH GRADE IMPROVES!

One thing I know for sure is that this year I'm only accepting store-bought presents. Last Christmas, Mom gave me a really nice hand-knit blanket, and I had that thing wrapped around me for half the winter.

But I found a picture of the same blanket on Great Uncle Bruce, who passed away a few years ago, so I pawned it off on Rodrick for his birthday.

<u>Sunday</u>

I was gonna play Net Kritterz all weekend,
but yesterday Mom said the amount of time I'm
spending playing that game is "unhealthy" and
that I had to interact with a "real live person."

So I called up Rowley and asked him to come
over, even though I was still a little bothered by
the whole skipping thing.

When Rowley got to my house, we sat down in
front of the TV to play video games, but Mom
said we had to shut off the machine and interact
"face-to-face."

But one of the things that makes my friendship
with Rowley work is that he doesn't MIND
watching me play video games.

49

Plus, the reason our ancestors invented technology in the first place was so they didn't HAVE to interact with one another.

Mom sent me and Rowley down to the basement, and the two of us tried to figure out what to do. I'd asked Rowley to bring some DVDs with him so we could stay up late watching movies.

But he only brought HOME movies, and you couldn't PAY me to watch THOSE.

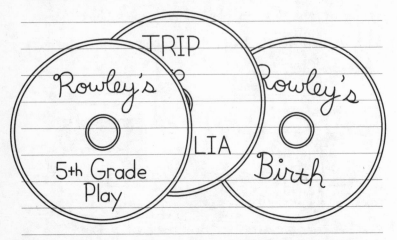

Mom brought us down some "Wacky Sentences" books, where you fill in the blanks to create funny phrases.

For the first round, Rowley came up with the words and I wrote them down in the blanks. The phrases we made were actually pretty funny, but what WASN'T funny was Rowley's new habit of saying "LOL" instead of laughing.

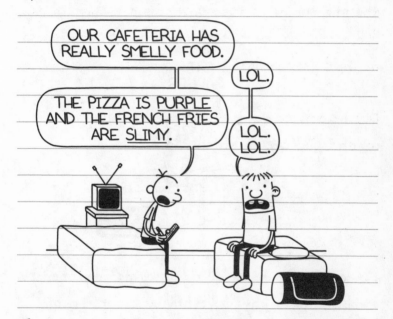

It was really driving me CRAZY. So we switched roles, and I came up with the words instead. Rowley started by asking me for the name of a sport, so I said "volleyball." But he told me it's "bolleyball," with a "b." So then we got into this huge argument about what letter "volleyball" starts with.

I found a dictionary and handed it to Rowley and told him to look it up himself. But instead of flipping to the letter "v," Rowley read every single word in the "b" section. And when he couldn't find "bolleyball," he started over from the beginning.

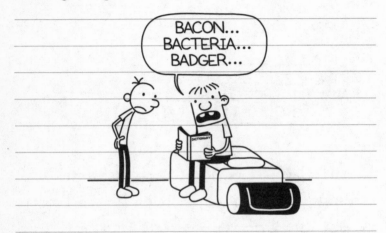

Rowley accused me of having an outdated dictionary and said that's why "bolleyball" wasn't in it, so THEN we got into an argument about what year volleyball was invented.

By this point Rowley was really getting on my nerves, and I realized we'd better change gears or we were gonna end up in a fight, as usual.

I told Rowley maybe we should do something different, and he said he wanted to play Hide-and-Seek. But the problem with playing Hide-and-Seek with Rowley is he thinks that when he can't see YOU, you can't see HIM. So that makes him really easy to find.

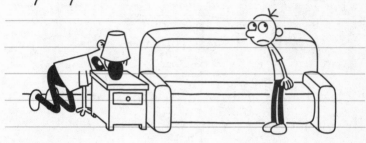

I decided we just needed a break from each other, so I came up with an idea. I told Rowley we were gonna see who was braver, me or him, and we stepped out the sliding glass door.

Each of us had to walk into the woods and write our name on the tree fort we built last summer. And whoever chickened out was wrong about volleyball and had to call the other guy "sir" for the rest of his life.

Rowley seemed to think that was a fair deal.

I told Rowley I'd go first, and I walked into
the woods. But as soon as I knew he couldn't see
me, I ran around to the front of my house.

There's no WAY I was gonna go into those
woods by myself at night. I had written my name
on the tree fort when me and Rowley built it over
the summer, and that's the reason I came up
with the dare.

I walked in the front door, made a bowl of ice cream, and relaxed for a while. And I have to say, some time to myself was just what I needed.

Once I finished my ice cream, I walked around the side of the house, rubbed some dirt on my face and clothes, then came running out of the woods.

I probably shouldn't have added that last part, because Rowley totally gave up on the dare after that.

Anyway, that break was just what the doctor ordered, and the rest of the night was argument-free.

This morning my family headed to church, and Rowley came with us. I don't think Rowley's family really goes to church that much, so he's not used to all the rules about what you're supposed to do and when. So I always have to tell him when you need to kneel and stand and all that.

Toward the end we all did the "Peace be with you" part, where you're supposed to shake everyone's hand. I said "Peace be with you" to Rowley, but he started giggling.

I think he must've thought I said "Peas be with you," like the vegetable.

I don't think Rowley totally understood that you're just supposed to shake hands with people, either, because when the woman in the pew behind us said "Peace be with you," Rowley gave her a big wet kiss on the cheek.

After church we dropped Rowley off at his house, and I was glad he was gone and that I could go back to playing my game.

And something tells me Mom felt the same way.

DECEMBER

<u>Tuesday</u>

Today I was playing Net Kritterz in my room, and Mom walked in. She watched for a while, then asked what I was doing in the game. I explained that I was watching my Chihuahua watch TV, because if your virtual pet watches at least two hours of commercials a day, it makes him happy and you get twenty bonus tokens.

59

Then I asked Mom if she wouldn't mind spotting me ten bucks because the Net Kritterz store just started carrying trampoline shoes and I was pretty sure Gregory's Little Friend would really like to have them.

But I guess I picked the wrong time to ask Mom for a loan, because it seemed like she was in a bad mood. She said I didn't have any appreciation for the "value of money" and that if I wanted to pay for my Net Kritterz "habit," it was gonna have to come out of my own pocket.

I told Mom I didn't have any money of my own and that's why I kept hitting up her and Dad. But she said there were PLENTY of things I could do to earn some. She said it's supposed to snow tonight and I could go out and shovel our neighbors' driveways tomorrow.

I REALLY don't feel comfortable knocking on doors and asking our neighbors for money. My school has three fundraisers a year, and I have to go from house to house begging people I hardly know to buy something from me.

And half the time I don't even really know what it is I'm selling.

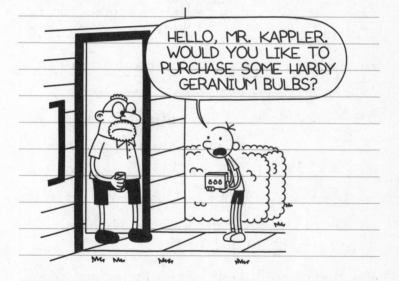

HELLO, MR. KAPPLER. WOULD YOU LIKE TO PURCHASE SOME HARDY GERANIUM BULBS?

I wish the school would give us something USEFUL to sell, like candy bars or cookies. The Girl Scouts are lucky, because at least they get to sell stuff people actually WANT.

The way the system works with these fundraisers is that us students do all the work and the school gives us these junky prizes as rewards. One time I sold twenty dollars' worth of gourmet coffee beans, and all I got was a cheap yo-yo that broke before I even got off school property.

But Rowley REALLY got stiffed. He sold $150 worth of beans and got a Chinese finger trap as his prize. It actually worked like it was supposed to, but Rowley couldn't get his fingers out, and his mom had to cut it off when he got home.

Last year the school tried something different. They had us sell raffle tickets, and whoever won the raffle would get a spring yard cleanup from the seventh-grade class.

Mrs. Spangler, who lives down the street from me, won the raffle, and on the first day of spring the whole seventh grade showed up at her house. But there were only two rakes for all those kids, so most of the class just ended up sitting around with nothing to do.

And by the time the "spring cleanup" was done, Mrs. Spangler's yard was worse off than when it started.

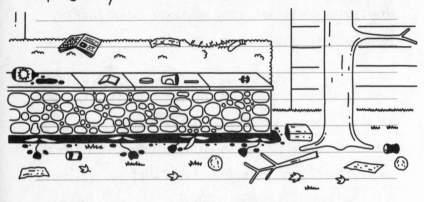

The new thing the school is doing is these Walkathons. The idea is that we'll walk around the track at school a certain number of times, like one hundred or two hundred laps, and get our neighbors to sponsor us for each lap we complete.

WALKATHON
Sponsor Sheet
$0.25/lap

Name	# of laps
1. Georgette Kramer	100
2. Tony Sinclair	150
3. Henry Nielson	50
4. Leslie Simpson	100
5. Barbara Preston	150
6. Lavar Collison	100
7.	
8.	

I can understand asking someone to pay for seeds or coffee beans or whatever, but I don't know what kind of person gets pleasure out of having some kid walk around a football field a couple hundred times.

The reason the school put on the Walkathon in September was so they could pay for a billboard near the town park.

KEEP THE TOWN
PARK CLEAN

I couldn't figure out why the school didn't just skip the Walkathon and have the kids clean up the town park instead. But I guess if the seventh grade was involved, they might've completely trashed it.

I've done the math, and I've figured out that each grown-up on my street gives me an average of twenty-three dollars a year for school fundraisers.

So I should just invite all the neighbors to my house once a year and tell them to bring me the twenty-three bucks in cash, because it sure would save everyone a lot of pain and anguish.

<u>Wednesday</u>

It snowed last night just like Mom said it would, and while all the other kids in the neighborhood were enjoying their day off from school, I was pounding the pavement looking for work.

I thought about whose door I should knock on first, but it wasn't easy. Mrs. Durocher lives right across the street, but she's a little too affectionate, and I usually do my best to avoid her.

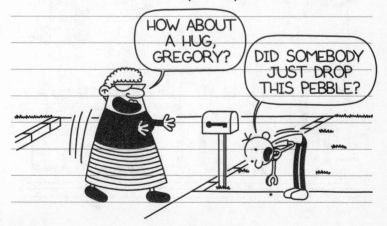

HOW ABOUT A HUG, GREGORY?

DID SOMEBODY JUST DROP THIS PEBBLE?

Then there's Mr. Alexander, who moved into the Snellas' house. He must not have worn braces as a kid, because his teeth aren't very straight. Unfortunately, the first time Dad met Mr. Alexander was on Halloween, and Dad must've thought his teeth weren't real.

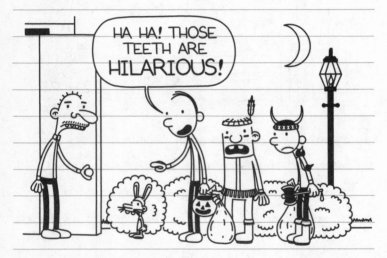

So I decided to skip Mr. Alexander's house, too.

There are people who live on my street that I haven't spoken to in YEARS. When I was about four, Mom and Dad had a cocktail party for some of the couples in the neighborhood, and I went downstairs during the party to use the bathroom.

But I guess back then I didn't know you were supposed to keep the door locked, so Mr. Harkin walked right in on me.

When I was done I found Mom and told on Mr. Harkin, and I'm sure he felt like a jerk.

So I'm not about to knock on the door of some guy I ratted out when I was in preschool and ask him for money, either.

Today I realized there's just too much history between me and the people in my neighborhood, so I decided to go one street over to Prentice Lane and start fresh.

I walked up to the house on the corner and knocked on the door. But I recognized the lady who answered. She was Mrs. Melcher, one of Gramma's friends from Bingo.

I told Mrs. Melcher I was trying to earn a little money shoveling people's driveways and that I'd be happy to do hers for five bucks.

But she told me she never gets visitors and invited me inside to chat.

I didn't want to be rude, so the next thing I knew I was sitting in Mrs. Melcher's living room surrounded by the lawn ornaments she took inside for the winter. I felt a little uncomfortable, but I figured if I was gonna ask someone for money the least I could do was try and be polite.

But all I could think about the whole time I sat there was how much money I could've been making if I'd just knocked on someone else's door instead.

I must've been in there for an hour before I was finally able to steer the conversation back to the subject of me shoveling her driveway. But Mrs. Melcher said her son was coming by in his pickup truck any minute and he plows her driveway for free. So that's an hour of my life I'll never get back.

I headed back out onto Prentice Street and started knocking on doors. I guess most people were at work, so it took me a while to find someone who was actually home. I finally got lucky when a guy who looked like he just woke up came to the door. I told him I'd shovel his driveway for five bucks, and he said it was a deal.

I got to work and was making pretty good progress. But it started snowing again while I was shoveling.

By the time I finished, it had snowed so much that you could barely tell I did any work.

So I rang the doorbell and asked the guy if he wanted me to shovel his driveway again for another five bucks. But he wouldn't go for it.

And to make things worse, the guy said he wasn't gonna pay me the first five bucks until his driveway was clear like I promised. See, this is why it's a good idea to have a contract before you start working for someone.

I got back out there and started shoveling, but so much snow was falling that I was getting nowhere.

Then I had an idea. Gramma's house was only a few streets away, and I remembered that she keeps her lawn mower in the garage. So I walked over to her place and pushed the mower back to the driveway I was working on.

I thought the snow-mowing idea was genius, and I couldn't believe no one had ever thought of it before.

Unfortunately, it didn't go as smoothly as I hoped it would. I thought the snow would shoot out of the side, but the blade cut right through it and the snow stayed where it was.

Eventually the mower started making funny sounds, and then all of a sudden it stopped.

So I guess those things aren't really built for cold weather.

RATTLE
SHUDDER

I pushed the mower to Gramma's and put it back in her garage. Hopefully it will thaw out before the summer rolls around.

I still had this guy's driveway to deal with, but now the snow was REALLY coming down, and there was no way I was gonna spend the rest of my day working for five bucks. I needed a quick solution so I could move on.

I could see that his garden hose was attached to the house, so I turned it on, put the nozzle to the "shower" setting, and sprayed down the snow in the driveway.

It was GREAT. The water melted the snow on contact, and I was cruising. Then I saw a sprinkler leaning up against the house, and I got an even BETTER idea.

Once I was finished, I turned off the sprinkler and knocked on the guy's door. He paid me my five bucks when he saw that his driveway was cleared.

I was pretty excited about the way things worked out, and I figured if I found some more people with sprinklers, I could have multiple jobs going at once.

Unfortunately, I couldn't find anyone else who was home. But my idea probably wouldn't have worked out anyway. Because by the time I walked back down Prentice Lane, the driveway I hit with the sprinkler was frozen over.

When Dad got home, we had to go out and buy five big bags of rock salt to melt the guy's driveway.

So now instead of having money in my pocket for all my hard work, I'm twenty bucks in the hole.

Thursday

Dad wasn't too happy that I turned somebody's driveway into an ice-skating rink yesterday, and he said he was disappointed in me for using "poor judgment." That's the exact same phrase he used a few weeks ago when I scratched up his car.

It all started when I won Student of the Week at school. When you win Student of the Week, they give you a bumper sticker that you can put on your family's car.

The bumper sticker is pretty corny, but it was still cool to win it.

My child is the
STUDENT OF THE WEEK
and I'm MIGHTY PROUD!

I'm not sure why I won, but I think they just give it to everyone eventually. Fregley won Student of the Week this past Friday, and I'm guessing it was for not biting anyone for five days straight.

Mom wanted to put my sticker on her car, but her bumper is so overcrowded that I knew it would just get lost on there. So I asked Dad if I could put it on his car.

Dad recently bought a new car, and I thought my Student of the Week sticker would look really sharp on his bumper.

But Dad said he didn't want to "junk up" his new car. At first I was disappointed, but I guess I could kind of understand where he was coming from. My family doesn't have anything that's really nice, and when Dad came home from the dealership with a sporty car, I was pretty surprised.

HEH, HEH.

Mom wasn't happy that Dad picked out a car without talking it through with her, though.

She said the car looked "flashy" and that since it only had two doors, it wasn't "practical" for a family of five. But Dad said it was the car he wanted, and he kept it.

After I talked to Dad, I didn't know what to do with my bumper sticker, so I just ended up giving it to Manny and telling him he could put it on his wagon or something.

But Manny turned right around and put it smack in the middle of Dad's driver's-side door.

I freaked out because I knew Dad was gonna think I was the one who put it there. I tried to peel it off, but they must use superglue on the backs of those things. So I got some soap and water and tried to SCRUB it off.

But after twenty minutes of scrubbing, I'd barely made a dent.

I started looking for different cleaning supplies in the cabinet under the kitchen sink, and I found some steel wool pads that looked like they might do the trick.

Those things work pretty good on the pots and pans, so I figured they were worth a try on the car since it was metal, too.

Sure enough, the steel wool made the bumper sticker come off the car as easy as pie.

In fact, it was so easy that I kind of got carried away. I used the steel wool pads to scrape off the bugs and bird poop, too. I figured Dad would be pretty happy I was cleaning his car for free. But when I rinsed the car off with the hose, I got a huge surprise.

The steel wool didn't just scrape the bumper sticker and bugs off the car. It scraped the PAINT off, too.

I panicked and started filling in the bare spots with a permanent marker. But the area where the bumper sticker had been was too big, so I wrote a note in Mom's handwriting and taped it over that spot.

Hi, honey!

Hope you have a great day!

P.S. Why not leave this note on your car so you can read it again tomorrow?

I thought the note might buy me a few days, but Dad uncovered the big area in no time flat.

Dad was really mad at me, but Mom came to my defense. She said everyone makes mistakes and that the important thing is that I learn my lesson and move on.

I owe Mom for that one. She calmed Dad down and I didn't even get grounded.

Dad took the car to the dealer to see how much it would be to get the paint touched up.

The dealer told him it was gonna cost a lot of money because it was a custom paint job.

Mom told Dad this was a "sign" that it was a mistake to get a fancy car in the first place and that he should just trade it in for a used minivan instead. So that's what he did.

The funny thing is that the minivan already HAD a Student of the Week sticker on the bumper from the previous owners. But Dad didn't seem to appreciate the humor in that.

Sunday
Our family usually goes to church at 9:00 a.m., but today we went to the folk service at 11:00.

The folk service has a different kind of music than the regular one, and there's a band that plays guitars and stuff like that. Last week Mom convinced Rodrick to join the folk group because she got a flyer saying they were looking for a "percussionist."

I think Rodrick imagined he was gonna get to play his drums in church, so he signed up.

But it turns out the folk group was looking for someone to play HAND percussion instruments, like the tambourine and castanets.

Rodrick tried his best to look cool up there in the front of the church today, but it's really hard to pull that off when you've got a pair of maracas in your hands.

I can totally relate to getting duped into joining something without knowing all the details. Last year Mom told me I should join the church's Pre-Teen Club, but then I found out they were really lax about who qualified as a "pre-teen."

Every year our church does this thing called the "Giving Tree," where people in need put their requests in envelopes and hang them on the tree. Then a family picks a random envelope, and whatever it says inside is what they're supposed to buy.

Adult male requests a scarf and a pair of gloves.

As far as I know, there aren't any rules about who's allowed to put a request on the Giving Tree, so I decided to try my luck and fill out a form of my own.

But something told me Mom and Dad wouldn't approve, so I made sure it couldn't be traced back to me.

Juvenile male requests cash, as much as you are willing to donate. Please leave the money in an unmarked envelope under the recycling bin behind the church.

P.S. Make sure you're not followed.

Monday
This year at school they taped off a bunch of tables in the cafeteria so kids with nut allergies could eat in a separate section. I think it's great the school did that, but it means there's a lot less room for the rest of us to sit.

I'm not sure anyone at my school is actually allergic to nuts, though, because for the first two months of this year the tables in the taped-off area were completely empty.

But I guess Ricardo Freedman liked the idea of all that elbow room, because today he plopped himself down in the middle of the Nut-Free Zone and ate two peanut butter and jelly sandwiches he brought from home.

Today we had a general assembly, and everyone was all excited because they told us we were gonna get to watch a movie. But it was just one of those educational films about healthy eating.

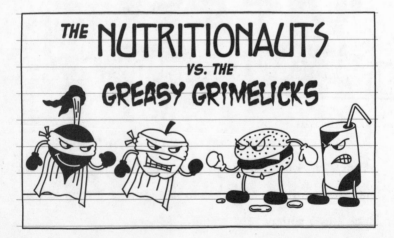

I know I need to eat healthier, but if you take fast food out of my diet I'm in big trouble, because I'm probably something like 95% chicken nugget.

The school has really been cracking down on junk food in the cafeteria. Last week they replaced the soda machine with a bottled water machine, but if they're gonna charge a dollar for a bottle of water, they should probably think of a better place to put it.

The school also got rid of a bunch of menu items, like hot dogs and pizza, and replaced them with healthier stuff.

They even replaced french fries with a new item called "Extreme Sports Stix," but it took everyone about five seconds to figure out that Extreme Sports Stix are just sliced carrots.

I usually bring a bagged lunch to school, but the one thing I would always buy from the cafeteria was a chocolate chip cookie. Last week, though, the chocolate chip cookies were replaced by oatmeal raisin cookies. I still buy them, but I eat around the raisins, which is a lot of work.

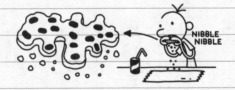

I can't tell you HOW many times I've bitten into an oatmeal raisin cookie thinking it was chocolate chip.

I have a theory that oatmeal raisin cookies were invented as a practical joke a long time ago and that they were never actually meant to be eaten.

Most of the kids at school aren't too bothered by all the menu changes, but the thing that really set people off was when they took away the energy drinks.

The reason the school stopped selling Rowdy Riot
was because teachers were complaining that the
red dye was making kids hyperactive. And if you
walked into my classroom after lunch, you'd see
what they were talking about.

But when they stopped selling Rowdy Riot, people
who were used to drinking three or four cans a
day were totally unprepared to go cold turkey.
In fact, some kids ended up having to go down
to the nurse's office because they had the shakes
from withdrawal.

The school wouldn't bring Rowdy Riot back no
matter HOW much people complained. But the
other day, Leon Goodson snuck in a backpack full
of Rowdy Riot he'd brought from home and sold
cans for three bucks a pop.

At recess a few kids who'd bought Rowdy Riot from Leon ducked behind the school and slurped down their drinks where no one could see them.

But one of the recess monitors, Mrs. Lahey, got suspicious and went back there to see what was going on.

Mrs. Lahey told everyone they had to pour out their drinks immediately or she'd report them to the principal.

But the second she was gone, the kids took off their shoes and sopped up the puddles with their socks.

Tuesday

One of the reasons the school has been getting on us about our eating habits is because the Presidential Fitness Test is coming up, where they measure you on all sorts of stuff, like how many sit-ups and chin-ups you can do.

Last year our school was in the bottom 10% in the country, and I guess the school is trying to do anything they can to turn that around.

(GASP)
(WHEEZE)

Grown-ups say there's a big problem with kids in our generation being out of shape because they don't exercise enough, but I don't think taking away our playground equipment is really helping matters.

In one part of the Presidential Fitness Test, they check to see how many push-ups you can do in a row. The girls in our class did better than the boys, but that's only because the girls get to do an easier kind of push-up.

The boys have to keep their whole body straight and go all the way to the floor and then all the way back up again.

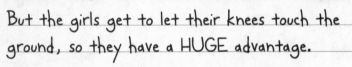

But the girls get to let their knees touch the ground, so they have a HUGE advantage.

Not all the girls were happy that they got to do easier push-ups than the boys, though. In fact, a couple of girls signed a petition saying they demanded to do the same kind of push-ups as the boys.

I'm pretty sure I know where they got that idea. In Social Studies we're learning about different ways people throughout history have protested to change things they weren't happy about.

TEA

TEA

TEA

SPLOOSH

I think the girls were expecting a big fight out
of Mr. Underwood, but he just told them they
could do regular push-ups if they felt like it. So
now we're all in the same boat.

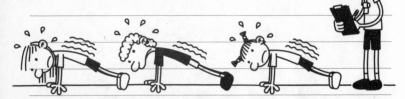

I thought that petition thing was a good idea,
though. I figured us boys should be allowed to
do the easy push-ups if we want, so I wrote a
petition and tried to get signatures.

But I got a bad feeling when I saw the group
of guys who wanted to sign my petition, and I
decided to just drop the whole thing.

A couple of weeks ago we had to do sit-ups during Phys Ed, but I got cramps and asked Mr. Underwood if I could just do the rest of my sit-ups as homework. He said that was OK, but he wanted proof that I did them.

So the next morning I got some of Mom's mascara and drew a six-pack of abs on my stomach. Then I made sure I had my shirt off when Mr. Underwood walked through the locker room.

The next thing I knew, though, I had a bunch of copycats, and the following day half the guys in my class showed up with their OWN fake six-packs.

But some of those guys were REALLY awful
makeup artists.

Still, I think we had Mr. Underwood fooled. At
least until we got sweaty and the mascara ran.

Wednesday
For the past few days I've been getting alerts
on my Net Kritterz account, and if I don't get
some Kritterz Kash soon, I could have a problem
on my hands.

MOOD METER

GREGORY'S
LITTLE
FRIEND IS
FEELING:

AGITATED

I asked Mom if she could just float me a few
bucks so I could get my pet's Mood Meter back to
"Calm," but she wouldn't budge.

Then she said I shouldn't expect her to give me
money to buy Christmas presents for the family
this year, either. She said I'm at the age where
I need to be spending my own money so that my
gifts "mean" something.

Usually Mom gives me twenty dollars to spend on
presents and I do all my shopping at the Holiday
Bazaar at school. It's great because I can get all
my Christmas shopping done in one shot and the
stuff at the Bazaar is dirt cheap.

So I always come away with a little money I can spend on myself.

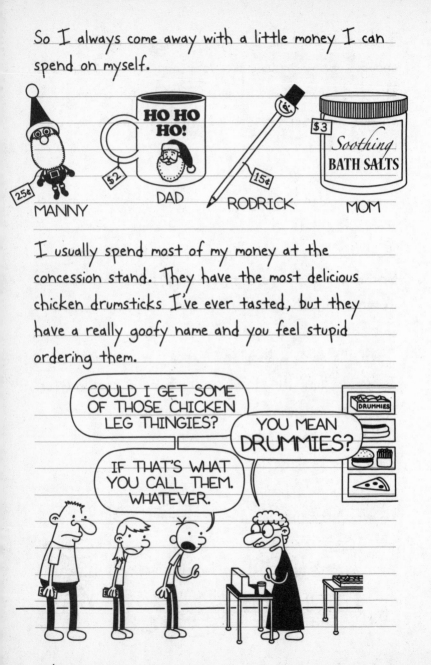

I usually spend most of my money at the concession stand. They have the most delicious chicken drumsticks I've ever tasted, but they have a really goofy name and you feel stupid ordering them.

I don't know how I'm gonna scrape together enough money to buy everyone a present. Basically, there are two times a year when I can count on getting spending money, and that's on my birthday and Christmas.

I'm just glad my birthday's a few months away from Christmas so I get separate gifts for BOTH. I feel bad for people who have their birthday right around the holidays, because it gets lumped together with Christmas and they end up getting cheated out of a gift.

It's not fair, but I guess it's been happening for thousands of years.

I realized something today, though. I might not have any cash, but I DO have something valuable: my first-edition signed copy of the "Tower of Druids" graphic novel.

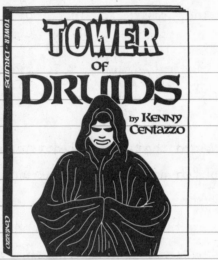

I got "Tower of Druids" signed by the author, Kenny Centazzo, at the comics convention in the city last year.

Well, actually, I didn't technically get it signed— Mom did. I waited in line for two and a half hours, and then I had to take a bathroom break. By the time I got back, Mom had gotten my book signed.

I was bummed that I didn't get to meet Kenny Centazzo, but at least I got his autograph.

I looked on the computer today and found out that a first-edition signed copy of "Tower of Druids" is worth forty bucks. So that'll cover me for Christmas presents, and I'll have enough left over to get Gregory's Little Friend that jacuzzi he seems to want.

I told Mom about my plan to sell my book, and she didn't like the idea. She said I waited a long time to get that thing signed and I would really regret selling it.

Mom said that when I had kids, they'd be mad I sold it because it'll be worth a lot of money.

Well, that settled it for me. I've already decided I'm not HAVING any kids. I want to be a bachelor like my Uncle Charlie, who spends all his money on vacations and heated toilet seats and stuff like that, instead of forking it over to a bunch of ungrateful kids.

HEY THERE, PLUMMERS!

I can thank my librarian, Mrs. Schneiderman, for getting me into the "Tower of Druids" series to begin with, because she's the one who started the graphic novel section in our school library.

I don't know when they started calling comic books graphic novels, but I'm glad they did. Some of the teachers complain that they don't count as REAL reading, but the way I see it, if they're in the library, they're fair game for book reports.

Unfortunately, when Mrs. Schneiderman put in the graphic novels, she got rid of the Easy Reader section. I always used the books in the Easy Reader section to do my reports for Social Studies, because you could whip through one of them in about forty-five seconds.

As a boy, Abraham Lincoln liked to read. He liked to read a lot!

When I was little I used to want to be an author myself. But whenever I started telling Mom my ideas, she'd say my story was just like some book that was already published.

I realized all the good ideas were taken before I was even born.

Mom said if I wanted to be an author, I should try coming up with something original. But it was really hard coming up with a fresh idea, so I just took one of my favorite books and more or less copied it word for word with a few small tweaks.

When Mom read what I wrote, she was really impressed, and I guess she thought I was some kind of genius or something.

But I think Mom got a little carried away. She sent my book to a publisher in New York, who told her I'd plagiarized "Geoffrey the Gorilla," which was already a bestselling kids' book.

Mom was pretty mad at me for passing off the book as my own, but I'm surprised she couldn't figure it out herself from reading it.

Geoffrey the Dinosaur swings from vine to vine. He perches in a tree and eats a banana. "Ooh ooh ooh," Geoffrey says as he pounds his chest.

Thursday

Well, it turns out my first-edition copy of "Tower of Druids" is totally worthless. I brought it to the comic book shop yesterday afternoon hoping to cash in, but the guy who works there told me the autograph was a forgery.

I told him he didn't know what he was talking about, because Mom got my book signed by the actual author. But the comic book guy showed me a catalog with Kenny Centazzo's signature in it, and it looked COMPLETELY different.

I was really confused, but on the walk home I realized what must've happened. Mom probably got tired of waiting in line at the comics convention and just signed the book HERSELF. In fact, I should've figured that out from the inscription.

Readers are winners! Keep reading to make your dreams come true!
                    Your pal,
                        Kenny

It wouldn't be the FIRST time Mom pulled this sort of thing, because she has ZERO patience for waiting in line.

When I was little I used to like to get my picture taken with the characters at theme parks. But whenever there was more than a five-minute wait, Mom would just walk to the front of the line and snap a picture of the character and whatever kid was posing with him. That's why our vacation photo albums are full of pictures of random people.

SNAP

When I got home I went straight to Mom's room with my book, and the look on her face said it all. So now I know why she didn't want me to sell it.

I just hope Mom knows that when she doesn't get a present from me on Christmas, she's only got herself to blame.

Friday
Even though I was still pretty mad at Mom for forging that signature, she bailed me out today. At school Rowley was carrying a present, and I asked him what it was for. He said it was his Secret Holiday Buddy gift.

I forgot all ABOUT the Secret Holiday Buddy thing.

Everyone at school is supposed to buy a gift for the person they get assigned and then give it anonymously.

The person I was supposed to get a gift for was Dean Delarosa, who I've known a long time. Back in third grade, I got invited to Dean's birthday party, but Mom got the date wrong and I showed up at his house a week EARLY.

Dean's mom told us the party was the following week, so we went home.

But the gift Mom bought for Dean was really
cool, and I ended up playing with it myself.

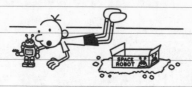

By the time Dean's actual birthday rolled around,
I'd already broken the robot's hand and lost the
gun that came with it, so I skipped the party.

I've felt guilty about that ever since, and today
I didn't want to cheat Dean out of a gift for
the second time. So when I got to school, I
asked the secretary in the front office to call
Mom and see if she could pick something up for me.

And she came through just in time.

The teacher started handing out the Secret Holiday Buddy gifts, and I got a jar of gummy bears. Finally, there was only one present under the tree, and it was the one for Dean.

Unfortunately, Mom didn't understand that the gift was supposed to be ANONYMOUS, so it was totally embarrassing when the teacher read the card on Dean's present out loud.

THIS ONE SAYS, "TO DEAN DELAROSA, FROM YOUR SECRET HOLIDAY BUDDY, GREG HEFFLEY."

Dean looked like he wanted to crawl under his desk and hide, and I felt the same exact way.

Saturday

I always thought the only place in the world where you could get Drummies was at the Holiday Bazaar. But today me and Mom were at the grocery store, and you'll never BELIEVE what I found in the frozen food aisle.

Now I know that I can have Drummies whenever I want and that they're TOTALLY ripping us off at the Holiday Bazaar. You can buy a whole BOX at the store for what they charge for three or four individual Drummies at school.

In fact, now that I could get my own Drummies, I realized I could run my OWN Holiday Bazaar.

But first I had to buy up the grocery store's supply before the school beat me to it.

Other kids in my neighborhood have done this sort of thing before. Last summer Bryce Anderson and a bunch of his cronies set up a restaurant for all the neighborhood parents.

I heard they pulled in almost three hundred bucks, and I know for a fact that one of Bryce's goons bought a brand-new BB gun with his share.

I knew I couldn't run a Holiday Bazaar all by myself, so I called Rowley and asked him to help out. We found some Christmas ornaments and some other stuff in my basement we could sell. But I figured if we were gonna compete with the school's Holiday Bazaar, we'd have to come up with better games than the beanbag toss and the ping-pong-ball bounce.

Rowley suggested a dunk tank, but I told him I didn't think Mom would allow that in the house. Plus, we had a dunk tank when we ran a Fun Fair in Rowley's yard over the summer, and it was a DISASTER.

We didn't know you were supposed to protect the guy in the dunk tank by putting him in a cage.

Me and Rowley decided it would be really cool if our Holiday Bazaar had a video game arcade. We didn't have the money to buy real arcade machines, so we got a bunch of cardboard boxes out of the basement to make homemade versions.

We started off with Pac-Man because we thought it would be pretty easy to make. In Pac-Man you've got a little character who goes around eating pellets while getting chased by ghosts.

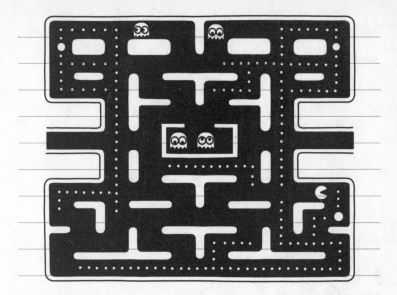

In our version we were gonna have Rowley on the inside of the box operating ghosts glued to pencils, while the person who was playing the game maneuvered Pac-Man from the outside with a popsicle stick.

We spent the next two hours making the box look just like the real thing.

But while we were working, Rowley started asking questions about how long he was gonna be in the box and what would happen if he needed a bathroom break. I gave him an empty two-liter soda bottle to keep in the box for when he had to go Number One.

Rowley asked what he would do if he needed to go Number Two, but I told him we'd cross that bridge when we came to it.

Once we were done coloring in our machine, we started cutting out the groove where the popsicle sticks were supposed to go.

But I guess we weren't really thinking ahead, because as soon as we cut the outer border, the whole maze fell inside the machine.

So I guess we're not gonna make a lot of money on Pac-Man unless people are willing to pay twenty-five cents to see Rowley sitting in a box.

<u>Sunday</u>
Me and Rowley still have a lot of work to do to set up our Holiday Bazaar, but I realized we'd better not wait until the last minute to let people know about it. So we went down to the town newspaper's office and told them we wanted to order up a full-page color ad in tomorrow's edition.

They said an ad like that would cost a thousand dollars, and I told them we could pay for it the day AFTER our event. But they wouldn't take an IOU, even when I told them how many Drummies we were planning on selling.

I suggested maybe they could just write an article about how two regular kids were putting together their own Holiday Bazaar and not charge us anything.

But they told us they didn't consider our Holiday Bazaar "newsworthy."

I think it stinks that the newspaper basically gets to control the information people are getting. At home, I complained to Mom, and she suggested me and Rowley start our OWN newspaper and write about our Bazaar.

I thought that was a GREAT idea, and we got right to work. We came up with a name for our paper and put together the front page.

The Neighborhood
TATTLER

Drummies Pricing Scam EXPOSED!

Tattler reporters have uncovered a price-gouging scheme at the school Holiday Bazaar that has been running unchecked for years. The popular chicken drumstick items, "Drummies," have been sold at the Bazaar for more than six times their retail value.

"I'm outraged," said a loyal customer who did not want to be
See DRUMMIES, A2

New Bazaar Offers Alternative to School Event

With the community reeling from the Drummies scandal, two boys have decided to make things right.

"We've decided to start our own Holiday Bazaar," said Greg Heffley, an entrepreneur
See **BAZAAR**, A3

We realized we were gonna have to come up with some more pages for people to take our newspaper seriously, so we started brainstorming ideas for other sections we could add. I figured we needed a comics section, so we started there.

T.G.I.F. — by Rowley Jefferson

Stinky Sebastian — by Greg Heffley

Ned the Napkin — by Rowley Jefferson

We added an advice column, where people write in questions about problems they're having. But we didn't have time to wait for people to send in real questions, so we just made a few up.

Ask Greg

Dear Greg,

My wife is always criticizing everything I do. The other day it was a little chilly out so I wore socks with my sandals. My wife actually made me go back inside and put on shoes! I feel like she treats me like a child, but she has a very strong personality and I'm afraid to stand up to her. What can I do?

Sincerely,
FRUSTRATED

Dear FRUSTRATED,
It's NEVER okay to wear socks with sandals! You should apologize to your wife immediately.

Greg

Dear Greg,
Are you single?

Sincerely,
THE LADIES

Dear THE LADIES,
Why, yes, I am!

Greg

Rowley was all excited about this newspaper, and he said he wanted to be like a real reporter and go out looking for stories. So I told him he should go around the neighborhood and see if he could dig up any dirt. But what Rowley came back with wasn't exactly hard-hitting news.

Kitten has a fun day

Mittens enjoys the nice weather yesterday.

By ROWLEY JEFFERSON

Yesterday Mrs. Salter's kitten Mittens was seen frolicking in her front yard. Mittens spent an hour and a half chasing after a butterfly that was flying around Mrs. Salter's azaleas, and when the butterfly flew off, Mittens got very interested in something that was jumping near the front porch. But by the time I got close enough to see what Mittens was chasing, the thing had hopped away.

131

I decided to make myself editor in chief so I could control the kinds of things we had in our newspaper. Because if Rowley had his way, our paper would be like a little girl's coloring book.

Mom told us we should go to some businesses downtown and see if anyone was willing to pay for ads to cover the cost of our first printing. The only person who was willing to buy an ad in our paper was Tony from Papa Tony's Pizza, and I'm pretty sure the reason he agreed to help is because we're in there at least twice a week and he didn't want to lose our business.

Tony gave us just enough money to buy some color ink cartridges, so we printed a hundred copies.

<u>Monday</u>

Yesterday we went around town trying to sell our papers, but nobody wanted to pay and we had to start giving them out for free. When we handed a paper to Tony, he didn't seem too happy that his ad was running next to a negative review of his restaurant.

Papa Tony's pizza stinks!

By Food Critic
GREG HEFFLEY

Have you noticed that Papa Tony's has started to really go downhill lately?

It all started when they took the barbecue chicken pizza off of their menu and replaced it with a spinach pizza.

Then they stopped selling grape soda. Papa Tony's was the only place in town you could get grape soda, so now I have to drink root beer, but it's really not the same.

And half the time the soda water doesn't mix right with the syrup, so you either get corn syrup sludge or soda water. I think they're just trying to give you a bad fountain soda experience so you'll pay for the canned soda, which costs twice as much.

My last complaint is about the napkins. You used to be able to use as many as you wanted, but now Tony only lets you have two, and if you take more he gives you a dirty look.

Papa Tony's
Two-for-One Deal

Order any one-topping pizza
and get a second one FREE!

*Mention this ad and you'll get an
additional dollar off your order.*

OFFER EXPIRES ON
DECEMBER 31

I told him if he bought a BIGGER ad for the NEXT edition of the paper, we could arrange for a more positive write-up.

We still had a few dozen papers left, and since we were handing them out for free, I figured I could unload them at school.

But when I started giving them to kids as they walked in the door, Vice Principal Roy asked me what I was doing.

He said I couldn't hand out an "unauthorized publication" on school grounds and that he was going to have to confiscate my papers. But I knew what this was REALLY all about. Vice Principal Roy was just spooked that we were gonna give the school a run for its money with our Holiday Bazaar.

I was still pretty mad about the whole thing when I got home this afternoon, and I decided I wasn't gonna just roll over and let Vice Principal Roy shut us down.

Even though Vice Principal Roy took our papers, I figured I could make some signs and hang them up around town to advertise.

I knew Mom kept poster board and markers in the laundry room for school projects, so I got to work. I used the neon green poster board, because I wanted to make sure you could see our signs from a mile away.

I finished making the posters after dinner and called Rowley to ask for help putting them up. We started with the school because I figured a lot of parents would see them when they dropped their kids off in the morning.

But right when we were done hanging them up, it started to rain, and the marker on our signs ran. And soon they were pretty much worthless.

But when we pulled them down, we got a huge shock. The rain had made the green dye from the poster board bleed, too, and now there were huge green splotches all over the brick wall.

We tried to get the green dye off the wall, but that stuff was like permanent ink.

I knew we couldn't leave giant green stains all over the school, so I tried to figure out what to do next. But right at that moment, someone yelled at us from the street.

Me and Rowley panicked and took off. We ran
across the parking lot and through the shortcut
in the woods, then kept running until we were
sure we'd lost whoever was back there.

I wish we didn't run, because if we had just
stayed and explained ourselves it probably would've
been fine. I don't know if the person who called
out was a parent or a police officer or WHAT, but
I just hope they didn't recognize us. Because if
they did we could be in some SERIOUS trouble.

Tuesday
When I woke up this morning, I thought maybe
everything that happened last night was just a
bad dream. But then I saw the newspaper on the
kitchen table.

The Daily Herald

Vandals deface middle school

Top: Juveniles left these green splotches on the school last night.

Left: Police sketches of the vandals based on an eyewitness account.

The suspects fled the scene when confronted by the passerby.

Vandals struck last night under cover of darkness and rain, leaving large bright green stains on the front wall of the town middle school.

The meaning of the green blobs is still unknown, but police suspect it could be gang-related.

"Graffiti artists have caused a lot of property damage in the past six months," said Sgt. Peters of the town police force.

SEE VANDALS, A2

So now I'm basically a criminal. Believe it or not, this isn't the FIRST time I've been falsely accused of a crime.

When I was in the Boy Scouts, I was trying to earn my Service Project merit badge, and I had to do some kind of good deed. Mom said I should go over to Leisure Towers and see if there were any elderly people who needed help carrying groceries or something like that, and she told Rodrick he had to give me a ride.

When we got to the parking lot of Leisure Towers, there was a lady walking around who looked like she was lost.

We asked the lady if she needed any help, and she said she was just walking to the supermarket on the other side of the apartment building. But I knew the nearest supermarket was almost five miles away in the opposite direction, so we said we'd give her a ride.

The only condition was that she had to ride in the back because I had already called shotgun.

We dropped the woman off at the supermarket, and then we went home. When we walked in the door, I was pretty excited to tell Mom about my good deed. I told her about the lady and how we gave her a ride to the supermarket a few miles from Leisure Towers and saved her a lot of walking.

But Mom said there was a brand-new supermarket
a block away from Leisure Towers and the woman
had probably been heading THERE. So that
meant we dropped her off five miles from where
she was trying to go, and now she didn't have a
way to get home.

Mom said we had to get back in the van and
see if we could find the lady, so we went to the
supermarket where we dropped her off. But a
cashier told us she'd already finished her shopping
and left.

We eventually found the lady walking along the
highway with her groceries.

We tried to offer her a ride back to Leisure
Towers, but this time she wouldn't get in the van.

I guess she must've called the local TV station to
report us once she got home, because that night
we were on the news.

This school vandalism thing seems a LOT more serious, though. Luckily the eyewitness sketches in the paper didn't really look like me and Rowley, so I thought maybe we'd be OK. But when I got to school, all anyone wanted to talk about was who was behind the green blobs.

The school had a general assembly in third period, and the topic was the so-called graffiti on the front of the school. Vice Principal Roy said someone had spray-painted the front wall and he was sure the perpetrators were students at our school.

He said someone in the auditorium knew who was responsible and that it was terrible to live with a "guilty conscience." Then he said he was gonna put a locked box in the cafeteria to make it easy for someone to leave an anonymous tip.

At lunch I could tell Rowley was really freaking out, so I reminded him that this "vandalism" thing was a lot of baloney and we didn't really do anything wrong. But Rowley said if he got a criminal record, he wouldn't be able to get into college or get a job and that his whole future would be ruined. It took a while, but eventually I convinced him to just stay cool and wait for the whole thing to blow over.

After lunch the POLICE came to the school, and Vice Principal Roy started calling kids down to the front office one by one. At first I was worried someone had identified us, but then I realized Vice Principal Roy was only calling the names of the worst troublemakers.

That's when I knew they didn't have any real evidence, and I started to relax.

DENNIS ROOT, PLEASE REPORT TO THE FRONT OFFICE.

At recess a kid named Mark Ramon told us what happened when he went in for questioning. The police had a machine that they said was a lie detector, and they claimed it was foolproof, so there was no point in fibbing.

LIE DETECTOR

Mark said it was pretty obvious the "lie detector" was really just a photocopier. But whenever Mark said something the police didn't like, Sergeant Peters hit the "copy" button and out came a piece of paper.

He's lying.

I guess the police eventually gave up, because after lunch Vice Principal Roy stopped calling kids down to the front office. So I finally feel like we're off the hook.

Wednesday

When I got to school today, I thought the green dye incident was totally behind me. So I was pretty surprised when I heard MY name on the loudspeaker during morning announcements.

GREG HEFFLEY, REPORT TO VICE PRINCIPAL ROY'S OFFICE IMMEDIATELY.

I walked into Vice Principal Roy's office, and he told me to take a seat. He said he knew I was one of the "culprits" responsible for the green blobs and asked me if I had anything to say for myself.

I looked around the room for the lie detector machine, but I didn't see it, and I decided my best move was to just keep quiet or maybe ask for a lawyer. Then Vice Principal Roy pulled a piece of paper out of the anonymous-tip box and showed it to me.

Me and Greg Heffley vandalized the school.

All of a sudden, everything made sense.

Rowley confessed, but he kept himself anonymous. I don't know if Rowley did it that way on purpose or if he's just a total doofus, but I'm guessing it's door number two.

I didn't see any reason to play dumb at that point, so I told Vice Principal Roy the whole story. I told him about the signs and how the rain made the poster board bleed and how we panicked and ran.

Vice Principal Roy thought about it for a while, and then he told me I should've come clean earlier. He said he was gonna have to give me a punishment to make sure I learned my lesson and said that after school I had to scrub the green dye off the wall with bleach.

Then he gave me a choice.

He said I could name my "co-conspirator" or I could just take the punishment myself.

Let me tell you, that was not an easy one. I really wanted to stick it to Rowley for writing my name on that piece of paper, but I also didn't see the point in both of us getting in trouble for something that I basically dragged him into.

So I decided this time around I'd just take one for the team.

And if Rowley gets into a good college or gets some dream job later on, I hope he remembers to thank me.

Thursday

It took me two hours to scrub the green dye off the wall yesterday, and it was hard work. I tried to get Vice Principal Roy to get me a few steel wool pads so we could speed things along, but he told me I needed to stick with the bleach.

I finally got home around 5:00 p.m., and there was a note on the front door. When I read it, I almost passed out.

> ### Town Police Department
>
> We came by, but no one was home. We will come back later.
>
> Sgt. Peters

I couldn't BELIEVE Vice Principal Roy gave me up to the police. I thought we were gonna keep this between us and that once I served my punishment, it was over and done with.

All I know is, I can't go to jail. This year they took our class on a "Scared Straight" field trip to the local prison. They had these prisoners talk to us about what their lives were like in jail, and it really freaked everybody out.

But it wasn't the idea of being locked up that scared me. It was the fact that the toilets in the cells are right out in the open.

I have a HUGE issue when it comes to privacy.
It's bad enough at school when you come back
from the bathroom and everyone wants to know
all the details.

I've never actually broken the law before, but
when I was little I THOUGHT I did. They
used to have this thing at my supermarket called
the "Cupcake Club," where they gave a free
cupcake to everyone under eight years old. I had a
membership card and everything.

Well, I kept taking a cupcake even AFTER I turned eight, and every time I did I thought I was gonna get busted. Then this one time an alarm went off at the EXACT moment I bit into a strawberry frosted cupcake with sprinkles.

Looking back, I'm pretty sure what happened was that someone accidentally tripped the fire alarm or something, but I was convinced it was for me and that the cops were gonna swoop in and place me under arrest.

So I made a run for it. Luckily Mom found me a few streets away, because as far as I was concerned, I was a fugitive and had started my life of crime.

But this vandalism thing was a whole lot more serious than the Cupcake Club episode. So when Mom got home with Manny, I didn't tell her about the note.

The person I was really worried about was DAD. I haven't been on his good side lately. In fact, this morning we had an incident I'm sure he's still sore over.

I was asleep when I heard someone knocking on the front door, but I didn't wanna get out of bed to answer it.

I was hoping whoever was there would just go away and come back later.

But the knocking got louder and louder, and the person out there was acting like a maniac. I buried myself in my covers and just prayed that whoever it was wouldn't knock the door down.

I thought about calling the police, but then I remembered I was a wanted man and that I'd have to deal with this problem on my own.

Eventually I got brave enough to go downstairs and grab a baseball bat out of the garage to protect myself.

Then it got quiet, and I pulled the curtain back to see if the person was still out there. But I was surprised to see DAD standing on the front step.

He had gotten his tie stuck in the door and had left his keys inside, so he just needed me to open it to let him loose.

So I'm sure Dad is ready to ship me off to juvenile detention the first chance he gets. In fact, if he's home when the police come, he'll probably hand me over into their custody without batting an eye.

It turns out I don't have to worry about Dad— at least not for the next twenty-four hours. It started snowing pretty hard around dinner tonight, and Dad called Mom to say it was too dangerous for him to drive home, so he was gonna stay overnight in a hotel near his office.

That means I've got until tomorrow to figure out my next move.

Friday
It looks like I'll have more time than I thought.
It snowed all night, and by the time I woke up
this morning the snow was three feet high. They
even canceled school.

Apparently we're in the middle of a BLIZZARD.
Rowley actually called last night to tell me we
were supposed to get a ton of snow, but I didn't
believe him.

Every year around this time, Rowley calls to
tell me there's a huge snowstorm coming, and
he's always wrong. His family taped one of those
holiday specials a few years ago, and the night
they recorded it a "severe weather" warning was
on the bottom of the screen.

So now the weather warning is a permanent part of the recording.

BLIZZARD ALERT: 2-3 FEET OF SNOW EXPECTED

Every time Rowley watches that holiday special, he calls me up and tells me a blizzard is coming. I used to fall for it, but I stopped believing him after he called me in a panic when he watched the special over summer vacation.

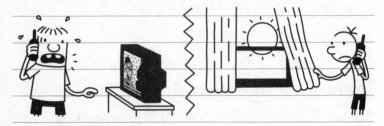

So it looks like we're snowed in. Ordinarily I would be really happy to be stuck in the house, because it would give me a good excuse to play Net Kritterz all day long.

But my account is locked thanks to Manny.

A few days ago Mom decided it would be a good idea to teach Manny how to use the computer, so she let him play on my Net Kritterz account while I was at school. By the time I got home, Manny traded in everything I ever earned in the game for tokens and then blew all of them in the Kritterz Kasino.

And the worst part is that Manny somehow figured out how to change my PASSWORD, so now I can't even play the game and earn my stuff back. For the past few days I've been getting e-mails from Net Kritterz telling me I need to get back on the site, but there's nothing I can do about it.

And if something doesn't change soon, I don't think my Chihuahua is gonna make it.

TO: Heffley, Gregory
FROM: Net Kritterz
SUBJECT: SOS!

Dear Gregory—

GREGORY'S LITTLE FRIEND
misses you!

Purchase more tokens
for your virtual pet
before it's too late!

This isn't the only password Manny has changed, either. He figured out how to mess with the settings on our TV and changed the "parental lock" feature.

The parental lock thing is supposed to allow parents to control what their kids can watch, but Manny changed the settings so that the only shows we can watch are HIS favorites. And he won't give up the password, no matter how much we try to bribe him.

Luckily I can still play video games on the TV. But Mom just got this exercise game, and now she spends an hour a day using my system.

When it got cold a few weeks ago, Mom said she wanted the whole family to use her exercise game so we'd stay active during the winter. I tried it out, but I don't really like to sweat while I'm playing video games.

The problem is, the game keeps track of how much you exercise each day, so Mom was on my case about not using it. But then I figured out I could use the controller instead of my body, and within a few days I had all the high scores on the game.

When Mom saw my high scores, she took it as a personal challenge to beat them. I feel like I should probably come clean and tell her I cheated, but she's already lost five pounds trying to get on the leaderboard, so I think I'll do her a favor and keep my mouth shut.

Mom always says I need to spend less time on the couch and more time being active. But the way I see it, I'm just conserving my energy for later on. When all my friends are in their eighties and their bodies are broken down, I'll just be getting started.

This morning Mom wanted to turn on the weather channel to see when the blizzard was going to end, but Manny wasn't budging on the parental lock, so she went into the kitchen and turned on the radio.

The weather report said we could expect another foot and a half overnight, which means this storm is gonna break all the records for our area by the time it's finished.

On the one hand I was pretty happy, because that meant I had some more time to figure out what to do about the police situation. But I was a little worried, too. The snow was already up to our mailbox, and it wasn't showing any sign of stopping.

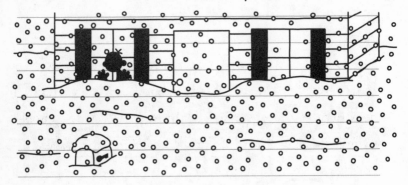

Mom wasn't stressed out about the snow, though. She said it was a good opportunity to slow down and relax and told me I should go down in the storage room to get a puzzle.

But there was no WAY I was getting a puzzle from the storage room. I have a big phobia about puzzles, and that's because once when I got one out of the basement, I opened the box and it was full of CRICKETS that had made a nest in there.

After lunch Mom said that even though we were gonna miss school, she was gonna make sure we didn't fall behind in our education. She said that two hundred years ago all the kids went to school in one classroom and that we could do the same sort of thing in our house.

But if I was in the same classroom as a kid Manny's age back in the old days, I would have gone bananas.

"B" SAYS "BUH." "BUH." "BUH."

Saturday

Last night Mom brought up some stuff from the basement to keep us entertained. She found a magic set I got for my sixth birthday, and all the tricks were still in it.

I never really played with the magic set because I couldn't read the directions when I got it. But today I read through the instructions and tried a few tricks out.

Hole-in-the-Table Trick

Tell the audience there's a magical hole in the table and that you can prove it by pushing a plastic cup straight through it.

Put a piece of tinfoil over a plastic cup and wrap it tight.

Slide the plastic cup toward you and allow it to fall out onto your lap. But don't let your audience see you do it!

Slap down on the empty tinfoil shell with your hand, standing up at the same time.

The plastic cup will fall out of your lap and onto the floor, making it seem as if it has passed through the table! Voilà!

The first trick worked pretty well, and I had Manny believing there was actually a magical hole in the table.

I really wish I hadn't done that trick for Manny, though. When Mom was in the bathroom washing her face, Manny got her glasses off the dresser and brought them into the kitchen to try the trick himself.

When Mom got out of the bathroom to look for her glasses, I had to tell her what happened.

Mom is practically BLIND without her glasses, so she said me and Rodrick were gonna have to help her out with Manny until Dad came home and she could get a new pair. Rodrick said he had some urgent homework assignments to work on, and he took off for the basement, leaving me to deal with Manny.

I had to brush Manny's teeth and tie his shoes, and then I had to make him breakfast. I poured some milk in the bowl and then dumped Manny's favorite cereal on top.

Well, Manny was upset that I poured the milk in first, and he had a fit. He wanted a new bowl of cereal since he said I did it in the wrong order.

But I didn't want to waste a perfectly good bowl of cereal, so I refused to do it.

Mom asked what was going on, and I told her
Manny was just being ridiculous. I expected her to
back me up and tell Manny to just eat his cereal
the way it was, but Mom said she wouldn't eat it
with the milk poured in first, either.

You know, back in the old days adults were
respected because of how wise they were, and
people went to them to help settle disputes.

FOR YOUR CRIMES, YOU
MUST REPAY YOUR
NEIGHBOR WITH THREE
HENS AND A ROOSTER.

Nowadays it's a whole different world, and half the time I wonder if grown-ups should really be in charge.

Mom went upstairs to take a shower, and after she was finished she yelled down and said there were no towels in the bathroom. So I got one from the linen closet and tried to give it to her. But the handoff was tricky because she couldn't see and I was shutting my eyes as tight as I could.

Later that morning Manny had to use the bathroom, and Mom said she needed me to go in there and keep him "entertained." But that's where I put my foot down, because I knew what she had in mind. Manny used to make Mom read to him while he sat on the potty, but it just escalated from there.

After Manny was finished in the bathroom, Mom said I needed to make him lunch. She said he likes hot dogs, so I got one out of the refrigerator and put it in the microwave.

Mom told me Manny is really finicky about the way his mustard goes on his hot dog, and she said he likes a straight line right down the middle. I didn't want a repeat of Manny's breakfast meltdown, so I tried to make the line of mustard as perfectly straight as possible.

I was pretty sure I got it right.

Manny had another temper tantrum, though. I thought the line must not have been straight enough, so I got a napkin and wiped the mustard off to give it another try. But I guess Manny thought that hot dog was tainted, so I had to microwave another one.

This time I tried to be extra careful with the mustard, but when I showed it to Manny, it was the same exact result as before.

Mom asked me to describe how I was doing it, and I told her I was making a straight line of mustard along the length of the hot dog.

But Mom told me Manny likes his line of mustard ACROSS the hot dog, and when I did it like that, he finally calmed down.

See, this is the kind of nonsense I'm dealing with right now. I've seen a lot of movies where a kid my age finds out he's got magical powers and then gets invited to go away to some special school. Well, if I've got an invitation coming, now would be the PERFECT time to get it.

<u>Sunday</u>

This morning at 10:00, Mom told me to go downstairs and wake up Rodrick. But when I walked down the basement steps, I could tell something was seriously wrong.

There was at least a FOOT of water covering the basement floor. I guess all that snow was too much for the ground to hold and it caused the basement to flood.

I told Mom to come downstairs quick, and when she did, she was REALLY upset that a bunch of our stuff was ruined. But to be honest with you, there were some things floating in the water that I didn't MIND getting wrecked.

Mom keeps a "memory box" for each of us kids, and mine was on the bottom shelf, so it was mostly underwater. One of the things that was in the box was my bed-wetting calendar from when I was eight years old.

Let me just say in my defense that there was a perfectly good reason why I was wetting the bed back then. In those days I drank a lot of water before I went to sleep at night, and then I'd have these crazy dreams that made me need to go.

OUR HOSE IS RIPPED! HOW ARE WE GONNA PUT OUT THE FIRE?

SLURRRP

I finally figured out what the issue was, but not before I got five frowny-face stickers in a row.

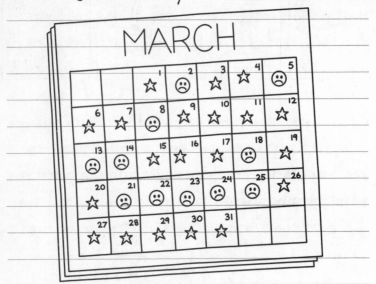

Some of the yearbooks from my elementary school days were soaked, but I didn't mind that, either.

My fifth-grade yearbook was in my memory box, and that's the one where we were allowed to choose whatever kind of background we wanted for our school picture.

I was the only kid in the whole school who chose "Natural Setting."

178

Haverly,
Jordan

Heath,
Olivia

Heffley,
Gregory

Henry,
Jared

I knew I should've just gone with a regular background, but Mom talked me into it when the forms came home from school.

PICK THIS ONE! YOU'LL LOOK SO RUGGED!

I don't really understand why Mom was so upset. Most of the stuff that got ruined was in the basement for a reason, and that's because we never USE it. One of the things Mom was really sad about was a "spoon carousel" Gammie gave us five or six years ago.

179

I think we were supposed to collect a spoon from every country in the world, but we only got up to Canada.

I did feel pretty bad for Mom when she found out one of the family photo albums got ruined. A few years ago Mom got into scrapbooking, and she spent a lot of time cutting out pictures and doing these really fancy photo pages.

But there's one page in that album I didn't like, because Rodrick always teases me about it. It's the one where I had a breakdown before a pony ride at the state fair.

HELP!

Gregory isn't happy on his first pony ride

Rodrick always says I was scared of the pony, but that's not true at all. I was scared of the guy HANDLING the pony, but Mom cropped HIM out of the picture.

PO
RID
$3

Speaking of Rodrick, the flooding didn't seem to bother him at all. In fact, I'll bet if I hadn't woken him up he would've kept sleeping even if his bed floated up the stairs and out of the house.

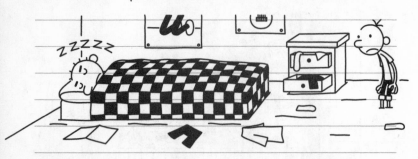

The rest of the day was pretty awful. The water in the basement kept getting higher, so we had to make a bucket relay line with some of Manny's sand pails.

Dad called from his hotel room to check in on us, and Mom told him what happened. Dad said he was really sorry he wasn't home to help, but something tells me he's OK with the way things worked out for him.

I would LOVE to trade places with Dad right now, because he's got a clean room and a king-size bed all to himself.

Mom told me and Rodrick that since the basement was flooded, we're gonna have to share MY room. She said it would be good for both of us to get used to having a "roommate," because it was practice for college.

Me and Rodrick shared a room this summer for a weekend. We had to spend a few days at Gramma's while Mom and Dad took Manny to a kiddie amusement park. Gramma has a guest room, so I figured one of us would sleep on her couch and the other would get the guest bed.

But Gramma said the guest room was "occupied," so we couldn't sleep there. She'd given the whole room to Sweetie, the dog we gave her. But you'd hardly know he's the same dog, because Gramma feeds him so much he looks like a tick that's about to pop.

Gramma said me and Rodrick could sleep together on the pullout couch she has in the living room.

But that couch is covered in plastic because she doesn't trust us kids not to spill something on it.

So me and Rodrick spent a whole weekend sleeping side by side on a queen-size pullout couch. I'd wake up every morning in a pool of sweat, and I don't even know if it was Rodrick's or mine.

I'm pretty sure that in prison you sleep in bunk beds, so if they lock me up at least I'll have a better sleeping arrangement than I did at Gramma's this summer.

<u>Monday</u>

After twelve hours of sharing a room with Rodrick, I'm thinking of marching down to the police station and turning myself in. Because there's no punishment they can dream up that could be worse than what I'm dealing with at home.

Last night Rodrick brought a bunch of his stuff from the basement and put it in my room. This is supposed to be a temporary living situation, but Rodrick is treating it like a permanent one.

Rodrick's got his drum set on stacks of books to air it out, and his dirty clothes are EVERYWHERE.

This morning when I was getting dressed, I put on a pair of boxer shorts that was sitting on my dresser. But by the time I realized it was actually Rodrick's dirty underwear, it was too late.

So until Mom did a load of laundry, I wore my Halloween costume. It was uncomfortable, but at least I knew for sure it was CLEAN.

This afternoon we were down in the basement seeing if there was anything we could salvage from the flood.

I noticed something strange floating in the water in the storage room, and when I picked it up I almost passed out.

At first I thought it was a real baby, but then I realized it was my long-lost doll, Alfrendo.

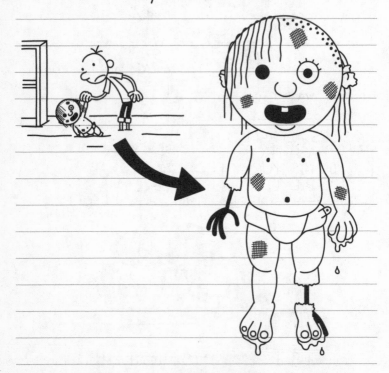

After all this time, Alfrendo wasn't looking too good. I think a mouse must've gotten to him, and spending a day in the water didn't help, either.

But in a weird way I was kind of glad to see him. I was living with the guilt of losing Alfrendo for all these years, and now I found out he was in the house all along.

In fact, I couldn't figure out how he wound up in the storage room. But I realized it HAD to be Dad. He was never really on board with the whole doll idea, and I'm sure he got rid of Alfrendo when I wasn't looking.

DOES ALFRENDO HAVE A RASH FROM BEING IN HIS YUCKY OLD DIAPIE TOO LONG?

I figured I'd confront Dad about kidnapping my doll when he got home, but at the moment I had bigger things to worry about. The first one was what I was gonna EAT.

Over the past few days we've been running low on food, and if this snow doesn't melt quick, I don't know WHAT we're gonna do.

Mom was supposed to go grocery shopping the day the blizzard hit, so we have less food than usual to begin with. She said we're gonna have to start "rationing" until she can go back out.

That could be a while, though. The snow is piled up three feet high against the front door, so we're basically trapped inside.

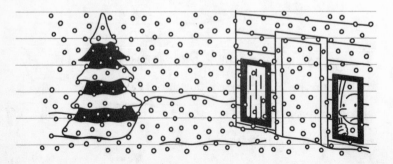

And Rodrick is spoiling the food we DO have left. He drinks milk straight from the carton, so there's no way I'm gonna touch that now.

I'm actually kind of mad at Dad, because if it wasn't for him, we'd have all the milk we wanted. A few years ago I won a contest at the state fair where you had to guess how much a baby goat weighed, and the winner got to take it home. I guessed the weight right, but Dad wouldn't let me have the goat. And if we had that goat, I could have a glass of milk whenever I wanted.

Mom found some burritos in the back of the freezer last night and made them for dinner, but they tasted funny, so I wouldn't eat them. Mom said I needed to eat SOMETHING, so I had ketchup as my main course.

Manny didn't seem to mind the burritos, but he'll eat just about ANYTHING as long as he's got his favorite condiment on it. When Sweetie lived with us, he used to chew on the furniture, so we sprayed it with this stuff called "Bitter Apple Spray" that dogs can't stand the taste of.

But for whatever reason, Manny LOVES the taste of Bitter Apple Spray, and to this day he uses it on almost everything he eats.

Speaking of Sweetie, I got so hungry today that I was seriously thinking about eating some of the dog treats I found in the back of our pantry.

But Mom told me they have different standards for making dog food than they do for people food, so that stopped me from eating any, at least for now.

I can't believe I'm practically starving here
while Sweetie is living the good life at Gramma's,
enjoying her home-cooked meals.

I only have myself to blame about the food
situation, though. We had a bunch of canned
food until a week before Thanksgiving, but then
I gave almost ALL of it to the Food Drive at
school. I got rid of the things I don't like to
eat, like yams and beets.

But I'll bet whoever got our rejects is having a pretty good laugh about it right now.

I was starting to wonder whether toothpaste had any nutritional value when I remembered I actually DID have something edible in my desk drawer.

When Dad wouldn't let me take the goat home from the state fair, Mom got me a giant gobstopper to make up for it. I spent the whole fall working on that thing.

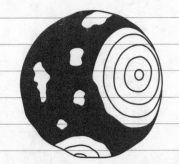

I figure if we DO run out of food in the house, that gobstopper will help me survive at least another week.

Tonight the electricity cut out for a few seconds and then came back on. Mom said there was a lot of ice on the power lines and we were probably gonna lose our electricity at some point.

She said if that happened, we needed to keep the freezer door closed so the food inside didn't thaw out and get ruined. She also said we'd need to keep the doors to the house shut so we didn't lose too much heat.

Manny got REALLY upset, and whenever he gets scared he hides in his room. One time when Manny was younger, I told him a witch lived in our basement, and he got really spooked. He went missing for a few hours, but we eventually tracked him down to his sock drawer.

Mom was right about the electricity, because fifteen minutes after her prediction, the power cut off and didn't come back on. She tried to call the electric company, but her cell phone battery was dead. Every hour the temperature dropped another two or three degrees, and we had to get a blanket to keep ourselves warm.

CHATTER CHATTER CHATTER

Manny just stayed in his room the whole time, and I'm sure he was scared out of his mind. I was actually pretty worried myself.

When you're used to having electricity and then all of a sudden it's taken away, you're basically just one step away from being a wild animal. And with no phone or TV, we were totally cut off from the outside world.

I would've felt a lot better if our street was plowed, because then we'd at least be connected to the rest of civilization. But I'm sure the snowplow guy is gonna come to our street last, because every time he comes up our hill he gets ambushed.

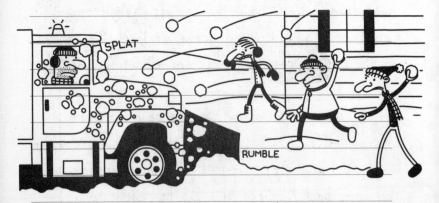

There really wasn't any point in staying awake, so I just went to bed, and Rodrick followed me into the room a few minutes later.

It was freezing cold, and I remembered a story I read in a magazine about these two guys who were stranded out in the wilderness and had to share a sleeping bag to conserve body heat.

I looked over at Rodrick and thought about it for a second, but then I decided my dignity was more important to me than staying alive.

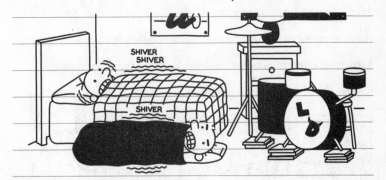

All I can say is, prison's gotta be a lot better than THIS. I'm pretty sure they guarantee you a warm cell and three meals a day, so when the police do come back, believe me, I'll be ready to go.

Tuesday

When I woke up today, I realized I'd somehow lost Alfrendo again, but I wasn't too upset about it. I was pretty happy to be reunited with my doll yesterday, but it hasn't been easy picking up where we left off.

SO, UH...WHAT'S BEEN GOING ON WITH YOU?

This morning I noticed it was snowing a lot less, but the electricity was still out, and Mom said we were just gonna have to adapt to our new circumstances until the snow melted.

She said I hadn't showered in a few days and I couldn't live like a "savage." I promised Mom I'd bathe TWICE a day once the electricity came back on, but she made me go upstairs to take a shower anyway.

The water was freezing cold, and the only towel in the bathroom was one Mom used yesterday. So I had to dry myself with some gauze I found in the cabinet under the sink.

After I got dressed, I heard a knock on the front door. I thought maybe the police had finally come to take me away, and I felt dizzy. But when I looked out the window I saw ROWLEY standing there, and he had something in his hands.

I thought Rowley had come to RESCUE us. But
when I opened the door, he told me he brought us
Christmas cookies, and then he asked me if I wanted
to come outside and play. I told him he was out of
his MIND and asked him how his family was surviving
without any electricity, but he looked confused.

Rowley said his family still had electricity and
everyone else on the street did, too. And sure
enough, I could see people's Christmas lights on
up and down the street.

Then Rowley asked me if I wanted to make a
snowman. I slammed the door shut, but only after
I helped myself to a few cookies.

I told Mom what Rowley said about the electricity,
and she told me to go down to the basement to see
if there was something wrong with our fuse box.

When I opened it up and looked at the circuit
breaker, here's what I found—

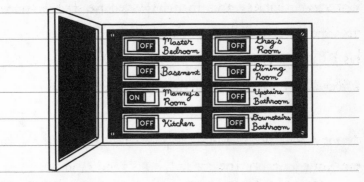

The only switch that was ON was the one for
Manny's room.

I ran upstairs, and when I opened Manny's door
I got a blast of heat. Manny was sitting there
with a space heater, a pile of food, and a bunch
of OTHER stuff, too.

When things got bad, Manny must've figured it was every man for himself. I think he would've let the rest of us freeze to death as long as HE had enough to survive.

Mom asked Manny why he cut off the power to the rest of the house, and he started blubbering that it was because no one ever taught him how to tie his shoes.

While Mom dealt with Manny, I went down to the basement and switched on the circuit breakers for the rest of the house. The electricity came back on, and the furnace kicked in. A few minutes after that, Dad called. He said the highways were clear and that he was coming home.

I looked out the window and saw the plow coming up our hill.

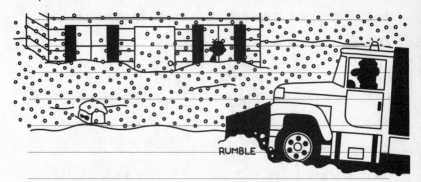

RUMBLE

Mom said it was a "miracle" that Dad was gonna be home for Christmas Eve, but to be honest with you, I had totally forgotten what day it was until that moment.

Dad picked up some food on the way home, and the rest of us ate like a pack of wolves. And let me just say, I'll never take food for granted again.

GOBBLE   CHOMP   SLORK
SMACK   CHEW
BITE   SMACK

Mom said she was gonna go out with Dad to try and find a place that was open that sold glasses.

Before she left, Mom asked me to take a present down to the police station for the Toy Drive and put it in the outdoor bin, because today was the last day you could turn a gift in.

But I wasn't too eager to show my face at the police station, and I REALLY didn't need to spend Christmas in jail. I knew I'd let some kid down if I didn't turn in our present, though, so I found a ski mask in our closet and headed out.

TRUDGE

TRUDGE

It took forever to get to the police station, and I crawled the last twenty feet to the bin just to play it safe.

Once I knew the coast was clear, I stood up and tossed the present in the bin.

Then I turned around and headed home. But when I walked by the church, I remembered something. I had filled out a request for the Giving Tree, and I asked whoever got my envelope to leave my cash under the recycling bin behind the church.

The church parking lot was covered in snow. I was pretty sure the recycling bin was buried somewhere behind the church, but I didn't know the exact spot.

Luckily there was a shovel leaning up against the wall, and I started digging to find the recycling bin. But it wasn't in the place I thought it would be, and I ended up clearing out a HUGE area looking for it.

I wish the church had a hose attached to the back of the building, because that would've made the job go a lot easier. I was pretty desperate to find that envelope, because I figured if I was gonna start my life on the run, I could really use a big wad of cash to get me by for the first few weeks.

But when I finally found the recycling bin, there was no envelope beneath it.

I was pretty bummed on the walk back home, and I forgot all about being careful not to be seen. So I was totally unprepared when I got to my front door and a police car pulled in the driveway right behind me.

I thought this was it for me, so I ran inside and locked the door. But when the police knocked, Rodrick let them in.

I thought about jumping out the back window
and making a run for it, but I'm glad I didn't,
because I would've looked like an idiot. It turns
out the police weren't there for me at all. They
were just there to collect last-minute gifts for
the Toy Drive.

I thought they might be bluffing and that they
were just using the Toy Drive as a way of flushing
me out. But I finally worked up the courage to go
to the front door, and I even brought a donation
with me and tried to act casual.

The police said they couldn't accept a used toy as a donation and that they were only taking new items in their original packaging. I actually think they were just a little freaked out by Alfrendo, because they seemed to leave in a hurry after that.

Christmas

When I woke up this morning, I couldn't believe it was Christmas and I was in my house with electricity and heat and wasn't on the run from the police.

I went downstairs to see if there was anything under the tree, but I was totally shocked to find there weren't any gifts at ALL.

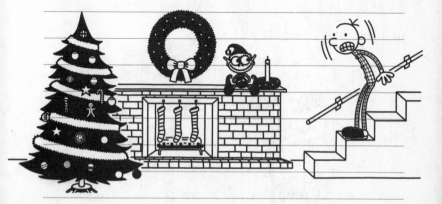

At first I thought it was all Santa's Scout's fault and that he'd been running his mouth about the trouble I've gotten myself into lately. But Mom came downstairs a few minutes later and told me Santa DID come last night and that he left our gifts in the garage.

Mom said the snowstorm really messed up Santa's schedule, so he ran out of time to wrap presents and just put them in garbage bags instead. That didn't make a lot of sense to me, but at that point I was relieved to be getting any gifts at all.

The rest of the family came downstairs, and Mom said we could have fun reaching in the trash bags and guessing what our gifts were.

It wasn't really the same. But I think Dad was pretty happy he didn't have any wrapping paper to clean up.

After I was done with the gifts in the trash bag, Mom handed me a wrapped present that she said was from HER.

It was my "Tower of Druids" graphic novel, so I was a little confused. Mom said she felt bad about forging Kenny Centazzo's autograph, so she found out where he was appearing a few weeks ago and got my book signed for real this time.

She said she had to wait in line for three hours but she was happy to do it for me.

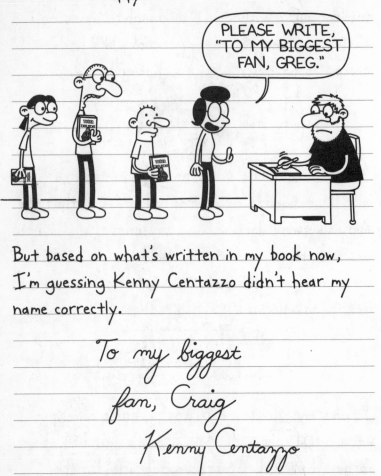

PLEASE WRITE, "TO MY BIGGEST FAN, GREG."

But based on what's written in my book now, I'm guessing Kenny Centazzo didn't hear my name correctly.

To my biggest
fan, Craig
Kenny Centazzo

Hopefully I can find a rich guy named Craig who's really into graphic novels so I can sell it to him for a pile of cash.

Rodrick got a snare drum and some drumsticks, and Manny got a bunch of toys and a pair of sneakers. Even though Mom taught Manny how to tie his shoes yesterday, it looks like he'd prefer to have her do it for him anyway.

After we were done opening presents, Mom said it was time to go to church. I told her we couldn't go because we didn't have any clean clothes to wear, but that's when she pulled out three last gifts.

I really like to spend Christmas in my pajamas, and the second you put on dress clothes, it feels like it's over. So I decided to put my clothes on OVER my pajamas and pick up where I left off once we got back home. But it was a mistake to wear flannel pajamas underneath corduroy pants and a V-neck sweater for a two-hour service.

After we got home from church, I went upstairs to change. I actually had puddles of sweat in my shoes, so I had to empty them out in the bathroom sink.

DUMP

When I got downstairs the newspaper was on the kitchen table, and here's what was on the front page—

The Daily Herald

Unidentified Do-Gooder Clears the Way

Unselfish Act Allows Soup Kitchen to Open

The blizzard that crippled the town and shut down many basic services threatened to cancel the soup kitchen, which many less fortunate individuals rely on for a hot meal on Christmas. But an unidentified juvenile spent his Christmas Eve shoveling out the church sidewalk to make sure that didn't happen.

See **MYSTERY, A2**

Well, the newspaper didn't exactly get the story right, but I'm not gonna complain. In fact, that article inspired me to put out a new edition of the "Neighborhood Tattler." And I'll bet we can sell a TON of copies.

The Neighborhood
TATTLER

Masked Hero
REVEALED!

The *Tattler* can exclusively report that the mysterious do-gooder who shoveled the church sidewalk on Christmas Eve is none other than our very own editor in chief, Greg Heffley.

"I just wanted to do the right thing," said Heffley when asked why he decided

See **HERO, A2**

ACKNOWLEDGMENTS

Thanks to all the teachers and librarians who have put my books in kids' hands.

Thanks to my wonderful extended family for all the laughter and love. We have a really special group, and I feel very fortunate to be a part of your lives.

Thanks to everyone at Abrams for making my dream of becoming a cartoonist come true. Thanks to Charlie Kochman, my passionate and dedicated editor, and Michael Jacobs for taking Wimpy Kid to ever greater heights. Thanks to Jason Wells, Veronica Wasserman, Scott Auerbach, and Chad W. Beckerman. This has been a really fun ride, and it's great to share it with you.

Thanks to Jess Brallier and to the incredibly talented team at Poptropica for your patience and understanding during the craziest of times, and for your dedication to creating great content for kids.

Thanks to Sylvie Rabineau, my terrific agent, for your support, encouragement, and guidance. Thanks to Carla, Elizabeth, and Nick at Fox, and thanks to Nina, Brad, and David for working with me to bring Greg Heffley to life on the big screen.

ABOUT THE AUTHOR

Jeff Kinney is an online game developer and designer, and a #1 *New York Times* bestselling author. Jeff has been named one of *Time* magazine's 100 Most Influential People in the World. Jeff is also the creator of Poptropica.com, which was named one of *Time* magazine's 50 Best Websites. He spent his childhood in the Washington, D.C., area and moved to New England in 1995. Jeff lives in southern Massachusetts with his wife and their two sons.

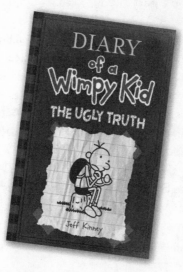

Greg Heffley has always been in a hurry to grow up.
But is getting older really all it's cracked up to be?

Greg suddenly finds himself dealing with the pressures
of boy-girl parties, increased responsibilities, and even
the awkward changes that come with getting older –
all without his best friend, Rowley, at his side.

Can Greg make it through on his own? Or
will he have to face the 'ugly truth'?

Being a kid can really stink. And no one knows this better than Greg Heffley, who finds himself thrust into high school, where undersized weaklings share the hallways with kids who are taller, meaner, and already shaving.

Luckily Greg has his best friend and sidekick, Rowley. But when Rowley's popularity starts to rise, it kicks off a chain of events that will test their friendship in hilarious fashion.

Whatever you do, don't ask Greg Heffley how he spent his summer vacation, because he definitely doesn't want to talk about it.

As Greg enters the new school year, he's eager to put the events of the past three months behind him . . . one event in particular he wants to keep secret.

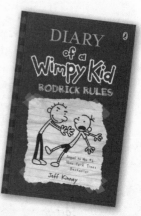

Unfortunately for him, his older brother, Rodrick, knows all about it. And secrets have a way of getting out . . . especially when a diary is involved.

ALSO BY JEFF KINNEY

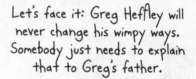

Let's face it: Greg Heffley will never change his wimpy ways. Somebody just needs to explain that to Greg's father.

You see, Frank Heffley actually thinks he can get his son to toughen up, and he enlists Greg in organised sports and other 'manly' endeavours.

Of course, Greg is easily able to sidestep his father's efforts to change him. But when Greg's dad threatens to send him to military academy, Greg realises he has to shape up . . . to get shipped out.

Greg, a self-confessed 'indoor person', is living out his ultimate summer fantasy: no responsibilities and no rules. But Greg's mum has a different vision for an ideal summer . . . one packed with outdoor activities and 'family togetherness'.

Whose vision will win out? Or will a new addition to the Heffley family change everything?

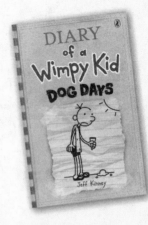

ALSO BY JEFF KINNEY

Packed with original art and all-new material, this Do-It-Yourself Book features ruled pages and empty word balloons so you can create your own stories and comics, list you favourites and least faves and keep your own daily journal. But whatever you do, make sure you put this book someplace safe after you finish it, because when you're rich and famous, this thing is going to be worth a fortune!

Ever wondered how they make a movie out of a book? Author Jeff Kinney didn't know either, but discovering how Greg Heffley and everyone else from his bestselling series, Diary of a Wimpy Kid, got turned into a live-action movie by 20th Century Fox, was an adventure he definitely wanted to share with you; so here it is!

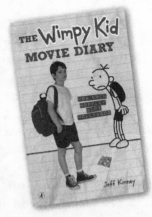